MW01686405

Crimson Shard

Joshua Kendal

JK

authorjoshuakendal@gmail.com

ISBN 978-1-0688297-1-0 (E-book)
ISBN 978-1-7381925-8-8 (PB)
ISBN 978-1-0688297-0-3 (HC)

For Them

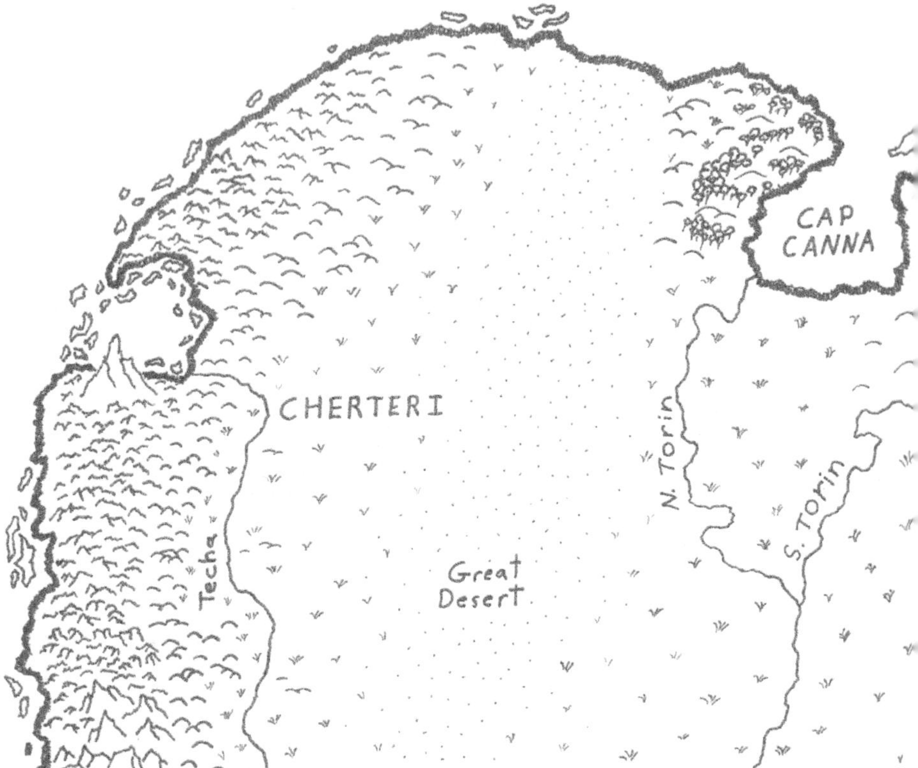
CAP CANNA
CHERTERI
N. Torin
S. Torin
Great Desert
Techa
RAICH
Torin
TENZIN
Whale's Bay
Greater Ice Flats
Kendle Isl.

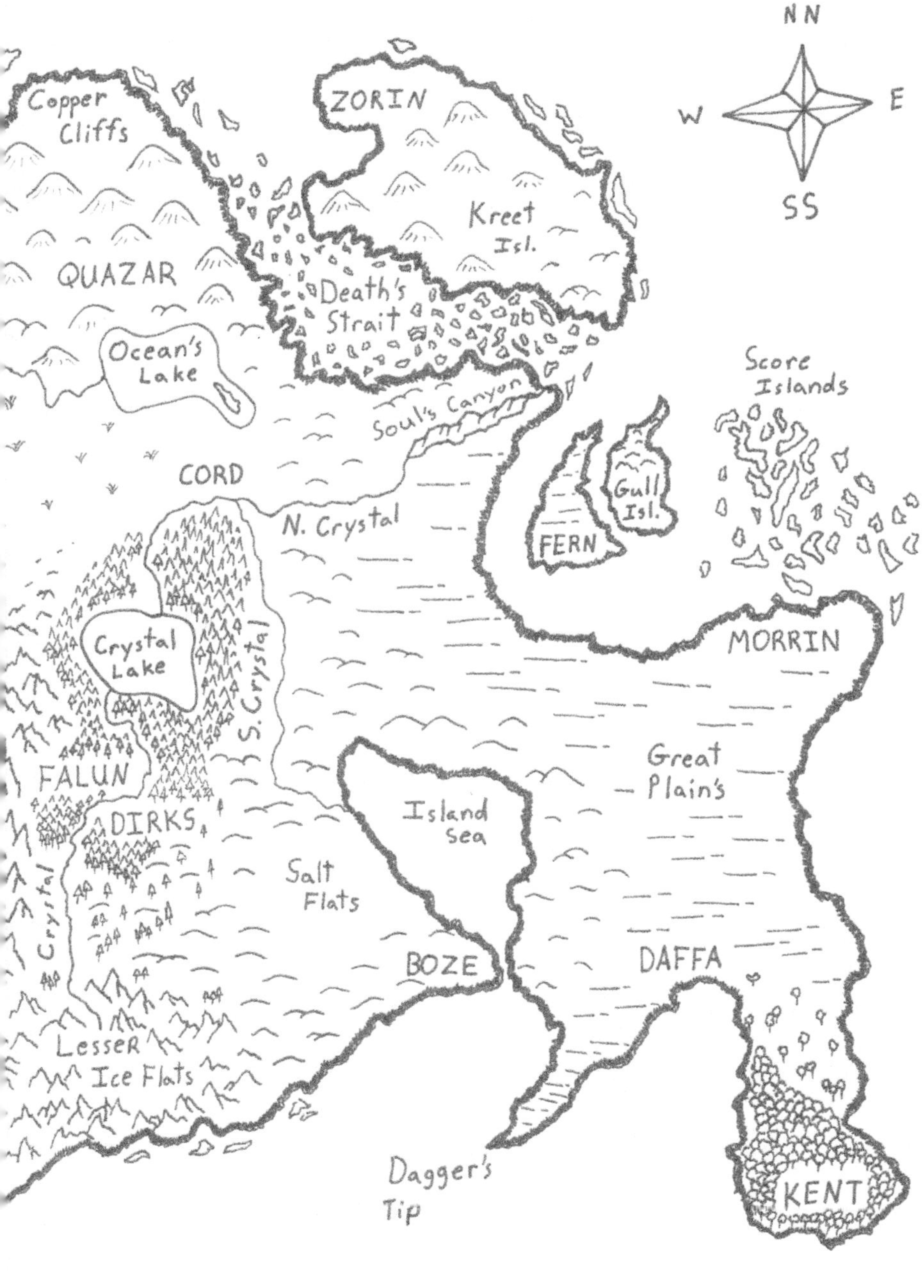

NN
W
E
SS
Copper Cliffs
ZORIN
Kreet Isl.
QUAZAR
Death's Strait
Ocean's Lake
Soul's Canyon
Score Islands
CORD
Gull Isl.
FERN
N. Crystal
Crystal Lake
S. Crystal
MORRIN
Great Plain's
FALUN
DIRKS
Island Sea
Salt Flats
Crystal
BOZE
DAFFA
Lesser Ice Flats
Dagger's Tip
KENT

Chapter One

Grasping the handle of his broadsword, Thor's knuckles whitened. He shouted, swinging his blade at a non-existent foe, and drove it into the remnants of the destroyed tavern's floorboards. Surrounded by only the breeze cooling his sweat and the silent city a stone's throw away, he dropped to his knees, enraged, his heart pounding within his chest.

"I swear," he grumbled aloud, sliding his palm down the blade. "I swear by blood. It can't end like this." Blood oozed between the fingers of his clenched fist to stain the wood beneath him. "I'll find Sorsha and tear that cursed Atlantean stone from her flesh. I'll free her mind."

He glared past the collapsed walls of the tavern splintered before him, and across the river to the foothills leading to the lone mountain in the distance. Towering like a tombstone marking the spot where Atlantis once stood, where he'd fought the Last Atlantean, where he'd last seen his cousin, Eric. He gritted his teeth. "I swear I'll find Lexa, bring her back to you, cousin. I'll put an end to this sorcerous plague yet."

A howl in the distance echoed in the silence, as if his cousin heard him, and responded. "You have my word, Eric."

Thor clenched his fist, digging his fingertips further into his palm, yet no more blood freed itself from his veins, no stinging traced along his hand.

He unfurled his fingers, red and stained as they were. There was no gash from his blood oath, nor a trace of a scar, only the callouses earned from gripping his broadsword in countless battles graced his palm. He stroked his short-cropped beard with his other hand as he studied his healed palm.

Had he been cursed, too? Like Eric. Is he, too, destined to turn into a blood-thirsty wolf that walks like a man when the sun casts her final rays?

Thor squeezed his eyes shut, recalling every detail during the battle with the Last Atlantean, Xanatos, and the seemingly unstoppable winged wolf under the sorcerer's control.

His blade had proven the giant winged wolf to be mortal, and at no point in their death match had it sank its teeth beneath his skin as it had done to Eric, changing him into a wolf. Of that he was certain. Thor breathed deep, concentrated. The creature's stench, its coarse fur beneath his fingers, and the searing pain in his side surged up as one.

He opened his eyes, examined his breastplate and ran his fingers along the gaping hole leading to his ribs where Kane's sword passed through the unnatural creature, and then penetrated his own flesh. No pain reached his mind. Only caked blood on his makeshift bandage ran beneath his fingertips. Tugging it off, aside from dried blood pulling his skin he felt no pain from the wound inflicted the night before, and no scar presented itself. He hadn't been bitten, but the sword that pierced his side was slick with the creature's blood.

He wasn't certain before, but now he was—the creatures blood mixing with his own had changed him.

The winged wolf's blood ran through him, healed him, and if his fortunes were the same as Eric's. Come sundown. He would turn into…a wolf.

Thor spun, screaming. He stomped over the splintered wall of the once bustling tavern, plucked a stone from the ground, and hurled it. The stone lodged, suspended for all time, encased in the cursed crimson fog billowing over Cherteri's unmanned wall—just like the people trapped inside the city.

Without Sorsha to lift the spell she'd cast, entombing the city, Cherteri's citizens would perish in a matter of days. The likelihood of her releasing them now that she has been transformed into a sorceress was small at best.

Thor cursed Xanatos and the shard of the Last Atlantean's amulet embedded in Sorsha's chest. He cursed the Raven, the woman the shard had turned Sorsha into. Though through no fault of her own, Sorsha had been altered so much that she became the world's first sorceress, an unheard-of feat as the Atlanteans ensured no woman would possess a power to match their own. She'd imprisoned the people of Cherteri in the very same fashion he himself had been restrained by Xanatos. He was freed from its clutches due to Xanatos's lack of concentration, that may be the same here.

He sheathed his broadsword, drew in a deep breath, and sprinted along the cobbles to Cherteri's main gate, testing himself. He had always been stronger than most men, and faster. He had not attained any additional speed like his cousin had due to the bite inflicted by the winged wolf. Sizing up the massive doors standing twice his height he took hold of one, and tested himself again against the slab of oak.

Normal operation took two guards to swing just one of the doors.

His muscles strained. The hinges creaked, and the door moved a hands breath, confirming the latch hadn't been set.

He was still himself. Perhaps he only possessed the ability to heal from a fatal wound unlike before. As amazing as it would be—never perishing from a blade piercing him—he despised the sorcery that granted him such a notion if it be true. He'd survived thus far with his wit and skill, and he knew his limits when it came to his speed and strength. That reassured him of what he could do, and more importantly, what he could not.

Thor had no love for the city, or its people. But for one to die by the hands of a sorcerer, especially without a sword in their grasp, is something that didn't sit well with him. He may be a sword for hire, but he still had his code, and an honorable death is a right every man should have.

The chance he could save those within the city by opening the gates and letting the cursed fog spill out were slim, but he had to try something.

Thor kicked his legs up to the other door, and roared from deep within his chest as he heaved at the defiant oak. The door swung open by a head, then two, then three. Using its momentum Thor gave it one last shove and backed away, prepared to leap clear of the crimson fog contained within the city surely to come billowing out.

Not a wisp escaped the gap in the gates.

Wide enough for even Thor's broad shoulders to slip between, the fog should be surging toward him, but instead it curled back in on itself as if riding a breeze that existed solely within the city's walls. Dense as it was, Thor could make out a single guard with his bracers crossed above his head, frozen stiff in his last vain motion to block the crimson fog that trapped him. Thor spat, disgusted by the sorcery before him, and his inability to free the people behind the city walls.

No matter the hardship before him he wouldn't complain or fall into depression. Those were not his ways. A man must act, and to act he must first have a plan.

He knew that if he were to fulfil his oath, and get Sorsha to lift the curse she put on Cherteri, he must first track her down. A difficult task even for him due to the winged horse she flew away on. Had she fled on a normal horse or on foot he could track her. However, even with the unconscious Lexa in tow, the speed of her mount was unmatched. He knew the winged horse's speed well, having used it to ferry himself, Sorsha, and Lexa back from the sorcerers mountain the night before. Sorsha came too, her alter ego of the Raven fully embraced, but Lexa had yet to recover from the blow she took to the head. Raven left the tavern, before leveling it with Thor inside it, with Lexa encased in a cloud of purple smoke. Thor had no doubt she would put up a fight if Lexa had regained consciousness, but it was doubtful she could slow their progress.

Which way would they have gone? Thor could only guess. He hadn't made it out of the smugglers hold that saved his life when the Raven collapsed the tavern on top of him to glimpse their direction. Thor had but only one course of action to take; choose a direction the Raven would have headed based on the experience, cunning, and prowess, Sorsha commanded.

Not west back to the lone mountain standing tall amongst its crumbled range. Not where her beloved Lucius died. Sorsha may have landed the killing stroke to Xanatos's heart, shattering his amulet of power in the process, but the wounds on her heart would be far too fresh to warrant her heading in that direction.

North to the coast would be useless unless she had a ship waiting for her. Though if half the tales of the Raven's adventures were true, she most likely had a ship in waiting, at least the means to procure one.

Thor huffed, disgusted at the transformation of her title.

The Raven, once Sorsha's chosen name earning her the reputation as the most feared leader of mercenaries the world has ever seen, was now corrupted. So resourceful was she that more than once tales had spread of her profiting from both sides of warring kingdoms. So tactical and deceptive she had convinced the world the Raven's exploits were concocted and carried out by a man, granting her advantages in both gaining information and retaining anonymity. But being possessed by that infernal amulet, Thor thought it unlikely she would have her clear wits about her. After her army was slaughtered at the mountain, she had no troops left to command, ruling out the coast.

That left Thor with two options: a four-day ride east across the Great Desert to Cap Canna, or south following the river Techa to Tenzin, where her army had once camped amongst its numerous foothills. An area she knew well enough to have concealed her forces just off of the caravan route. Not an easy feat due to their numbers. That was the same camp he discovered Sorsha was the great mercenary leader, the Raven. Yet the desert to the east was where he first met her. He grinned. Not entirely from the vision of her naked upon their first meeting, but also due to her prowess in battle she displayed against the bandits who had captured her.

Either direction was an option. The winged horse had no water nor food stowed in its satchels, and there was nothing remaining of the tavern to pillage for supplies. Sorsha and Lexa were out of sight faster than he could emerge from the smugglers hold, making a quick stop in Cherteri to fetch the supplies needed to cross the desert impossible before she cursed the city.

Possessed by the shard of that sorcerous' amulet would not push Sorsha to make an ill-supplied journey across the desert, of that, he was sure.

South it is, he decided.

His direction set, he went on to the next task, scavenging what he could to make the journey. Cherteri would offer nothing to him save entrapment if he dared to venture inside. So he turned back to what remained of the tavern, the Red Ox, the only building outside the high walls of Cherteri. Once a smugglers haven, the tavern was left alone by the city guard through heavy bribes by the owner. Its location bore prosperous trade, an entertaining crowd, and access to the crossroads of the caravan route. The westerly rout left Cherteri's gates, crossed the great river Techa, then split to either Tenzin or the now sunken Atlantis. The Northern route led from the Red Ox directly to the bay, where the world gained access to Cherteri.

Turning on the Northern route it took only fifty paces for Thor to nod to himself, and his reasoning that there might be something left for him to scavenge from the docks. Squinting as he strode, the bay and what remained of its occupants came into focus. He grinned as he spotted his means to keep pace with Sorsha's winged horse—Lucius's ship.

Bobbing in the bay, alone, save for its torched brethren lying beneath the water, was the massive ship outfitted with pullies, ropes, and a reinforced mast with a long arm able to swing over the side of the ship's hull.

A masterpiece of engineering the likes of which the world has never seen before.

Lucius's words repeated in Thor's head.

Though Lucius had fallen in the battle that brought down Xanatos, that would not be what Thor carried with him as the main memory of his friend. An oddity of a man to say the least. Cunning, far from humble proclaiming to be the world's greatest tactician, of which Thor had seen the evidence of being true. Perhaps his greatest strength wasn't how he won Sorsha's heart, but how he broke through her stern composure and evaded her sharp tongue—of which she spared Thor not one of its lashings—he wasn't sure.

Truly, the ship he approached as he reminisced was a masterpiece, for he had never heard of a ship able to wrench boulders the size of wagons from the depths of a river; not until Lucius designed the means to clear the debris blocking the river's mouth to the ocean from the destruction of Atlantis.

Stepping on board, he was surprised to find a covered wagon along with a team of six horses. If his one-time cell mate, Lucius, had accomplished what he said he had—of which there was no doubt in Thor's mind—then the reinforced wagon should be filled with untold wealth. Thor flipped back the canvas to a mountain of gold coins liberated from the King of Cherteri's coffers. Stretching to every corner and piled so high there wasn't room for a man to kneel on the coins without having to crouch from hitting his head on the canvas roof. A lifetime of trade with Atlantis had made the King rich beyond comparison, and Lucius had engineered how to steal it. All of it.

Thor dropped the canvas flap. He had come to Cherteri to ply his trade, seeking employment with the Raven, and become wealthy. He'd only herd tales of the Raven's exploits, and of his honor. Another reason he sought to be a sword for hire under his command, if only temporarily for the sheer adventure sure to accompany such a legend. That was before discovering the Raven was a woman, and that woman was Sorsha. The notion of hiring his sword out vanished when the plague of sorcery hit. He still wasn't certain if his and Sorsha's personalities could have ceased dueling with each other long enough to improve their fortunes.

That was his past, and now thanks to Sorsha, Lucius, Eric, and Lexa, he could live like royalty. With the gold in the wagon, he could buy a city, a kingdom, one far from the mountain that bore Xanatos's lair standing as a constant reminder of the devastation wrought upon the land. Still, despite a life of luxury set out before him, he had an oath to fulfill, and the setting sun weighed on him.

He needed to know, to be certain, that he would stay in command of his body; and his actions.

He clenched his fist where his blood-oath wound should have been, and hoped that he would not turn with the coming night. But hope was for fools, and he was no fool. Only those prepared for the trial's life set before them would survive in the world. His thirty-four summers—along with his speed, strength, and skill with a blade—had proven he was a survivor.

Rummaging in the ship's hold, Thor found what he sought: shackles and chains of iron. He stripped naked, placed his broadsword atop his breastplate, and leaving the key to the shackles within reach, bound himself to the ship's upgraded mast. He had witnessed Eric's power when he turned into his wolf form. He was confident enough that the thick oak of the mast could withstand an onslaught of a wolf's attempt to free itself in the event he too turned furry with a maw full of fangs.

He tugged at the cold iron weighing down his ankles and wrists. Satisfied he was restrained, he sat and let the coming night prompt bumps from his flesh.

The sun's final rays, silhouetting the lone mountain, faded beneath the ocean.

Thor pulled the cool night air into his chest, and waited.

Stars spackled the black above, and his only light was that of the rising moon. Cautious to not give his position away to any still alive, he had not lit a single lantern.

After what Thor decided was a full turn of the glass, he unshackled himself and rose. Certain he would remain in his true form, and not turn into a wolf that moved like a man, he donned his breeches, boots, shirt, leather breastplate and matching bracers. He had been cursed differently than his cousin. He could heal, fast, but as of yet he hadn't discovered anything else the winged wolf had passed onto him, and that suited him fine. Still, he had to test himself, to see if he was different during the night.

He concentrated, drinking in his surroundings.

The river feeding the bay seemed to churn up its dull constant drone as always. Cherteri, although dark within, stood hazy against the desert behind it; as it should at this distance.

Convinced his hearing and sight remained unchanged he turned his back to the city and focused.

Beyond the deck's rail, past the river, deep within the foothills on the path leading to Atlantis's final resting place, a single torch flickered in the night breeze.

Chapter Two

Thor studied the approaching torch from the deck's rail of Lucius's ship, and gauged its pace; whoever bore it should make the river's edge when the sun reaches its zenith the next day. Due to the torch bearer's distance and the collapsed bridge deck—the only way to cross the river—Thor was confident he could rest with his back against the ship's hull, secluded in the shadows, and not be detected. The torch bearer would have to travel all night and cross what remained of the bridge's rails to make his side of the river, a task not easily accomplished by those with even the surest of footing. Thor was safe from the stranger at the moment and shut his eyes.

Rising before the sun, and having checked the flickering torch's position throughout the night; Thor went about the task of preparing the ship to set sail. It was fully stocked with jarred fruit, dried meat, and casks of fine wine—Lucius had an affinity for wine, as did Thor—no doubt brought from Lucius's sanctuary. Thor had all he needed to weigh anchor.

Upon further inspection the furled sails appeared in tact, as did the rigging. Lucius's ship was the only one that survived the fire that decimated the ships docked in the bay when Xanatos first attacked Cherteri. His fortunes were improving with every step along the ship, until he inspected the mast.

Its swing arm was out of commission, pinned in place with iron bars thick as Thor's wrist, and locked in place. He chuckled; the wagon could not be hoisted from the ship onto land. Lucius's doing to ensure the gold remained where he had left it, no doubt. That issue he could work at on the trip to Tenzin, and if he failed to free the mast from its stationary position he could relocate the gold by hand.

The wheel, he discovered would spin endlessly with no resistance and required immediate attention. In the ships bowels Thor found the reason, the rudder chain had been disconnected from the wheel and chained to an iron plate. The locks securing it were thick enough it would take a great deal of prying from a hot iron to break them.

Thor gathered and hauled timber from what remained of the destroyed tavern, the Red Ox, left flat as the land surrounding it thanks to the Raven's outburst. He piled the splintered wood on the shore beside the dock, and set his flint to it. The wine saturated floor-boards of the tavern caught fire best, and the flames rose high above Thor's head. The fire would have to grow hot enough to make Thor's poker turn white-hot if he had a chance at getting it along the deck, across the foot walk, and into the bowels of the ship to pry at the locks.

Mesmerized by flames dancing across timbers, Thor allowed himself a moment of peace. Until he looked past the fire to Cherteri, recalled its people encased in their foggy tomb, and their faces frozen with the terror in their hearts.

Thor gritted his teeth, grabbed the poker from the fire and sprinted up the foot walk to the ship.

"That...won't...work!"

Thor skidded to a halt, brandishing the poker like he would his broadsword even though the voice came from across the river. He leaned over the deck's rail.

A broad-shouldered figure bearing a quiver and a mass of steel on his hip stood on the river-bank, waving. He donned a hat with a hard peak like that overhanging a doorway while the rest of it fit snugly against his head.

"Lucius!" Thor pumped his fist in the air, and tossed his poker, letting it sizzle in defiance of the water it submerged beneath.

"Key!" Lucius shouted, his voice dissipating across the hundred and fifty paces of the great River Techa rolling upon itself and circulating through the bay. "Wagon...slat under seat."

Thor nodded, though Lucius might not have been able to catch his response at such a distance. How the self-proclaimed *World's Greatest Tactician* had survived Xanatos's lair collapsing down around him, Thor didn't know. There would be time for swapping tales once he got the ship to the other side of the river and collected Lucius.

Lucius kept shouting, but in his excitement his words ran together in a jumbled phrase as Thor slid his fingers along the wagon's bench, searching for a depression or slit to unlatch Lucius's hidden compartment containing the key to unlock the rudder and mast. After more than a few breaths, and frustration setting in, Thor put his heel to work splintering the bench open with a single kick.

A clang of metal on wood rang out.

On the deck was a key. Made of blackened steel and large enough to match the oversized locks Lucius had installed.

Thor, proud he sidestepped Lucius's puzzle, held up the key and made to wave it at Lucius.

But Lucius was no longer on the river's bank. He was sprinting along the narrow rail spanning the supports of the bridge. Thor had done the same to save his hide from plunging into the river and being swept away when he'd charged into battle against Xanatos's unnatural creations.

Lucius moved as sure-footed as a mountain goat; not something Thor had known the man to be. Lucius reached the cobbles, and instead of turning for the ship, he continued East, past the northern caravan route to the bay.

"Where are you going?"

With no reply from Lucius other than a hand waving away his question, Thor gave pursuit down the foot walk, along the dock, and past the bay. As fast as he was, Thor couldn't keep pace until Lucius fell to his knees on the remnants of the Red Ox.

"What gives, man? I've nare had trouble running down…" Thor's words caught in his throat. Lucius's skin was pale and had a gray undertone to it. In a heartbeat, Thor knew why.

Xanatos had cursed Lucius before he died.

Thor was fast, and found it challenging in all his travels to meet a man that could best him in speed or strength. But the curse Xanatos had placed on those he enslaved left them with enhanced speed and strength that put Thor to the test like few had. The curse had another portion not so becoming, all enslaved lost their soul to the sorcerer, ensuring unwavering obedience. "Lucius."

"I know…I'm one of them."

The one-time cell mates looked at each other in silence for a moment. There was nothing more to be said of the matter. Lucius's soul had been imprisoned within the amulet, along with those of countless others. Some comfort came to Thor, in knowing that at the least Lucius could not be commanded against his will from a dead sorcerer, he was still a free man.

"Sorry," Lucius broke the silence after catching his breath. "Not sure why, but I was compelled to come to the Ox, to this very spot." Lucius slid his palm across the floor boards, stood, and eyed the ship. "Leaving with my gold, are you?"

"Payment for deceiving me into thinking you'd perished." Thor took Lucius's wrist in his palm, shaking it.

"I nearly did, if it wasn't for a slab of stone twice your height that sheltered me and left a rabbit hole as a chance to free myself. Digging out would have gone a lot easier had you stuck around to remove the debris from the other side."

"Would have had I known, but your fortunes looked to have run out, and I had to tend to the others."

Lucius looked to the ship again, furrowed his brow.

There was plenty to tell his friend about what had transpired since Thor had come down the mountain. How Eric, thinking Lexa to be dead, disappeared south into the forest still in his wolf form. How Thor hauled Lexa and Sorsha down the mountain to their camp, procured her winged horse and made their way to the Red Ox, Lucius's favorite tavern. How Sorsha had a shard of the amulet embedded in her chest, and how it transformed her from the fiery red-head with a distaste for men into a sorceress that leveled the tavern and imprisoned Cherteri before leaving with the unconscious Lexa. Lucius, being a methodical planner would want to know everything, would not want to be spared a single detail, and such a lengthy tale required plenty of wine. "I'll fill you in on our way to Tenzin. Fetch the finest wine you've stashed below. I'll drop her sails. We have some catching up to do."

"Tenzin, eh? I've heard it has a tavern or two that might live up to our demands."

"Just two?"

"I have very particular tastes." Lucius grinned.

Thor knew what Lucius preferred. Musty old taverns filled with patrons from across the land, all dicing and drinking their fortunes away. Tenzin was a city built to be one sprawling tavern. More than one man had left that city with an empty purse and a throbbing head. "I can find you enough adventure, and wine, to quench even your cravings."

"None will compare to the Ox." Lucius flipped over a floorboard of the destroyed tavern with his boot. "Care to place a wager?"

"I've traveled far. Seen more than most. Lived more than most. I'll take that bet." Thor accepted Lucius' jest with not a mention of coin. Gold no longer mattered, they had more than enough than either of them could spend in a lifetime. But watching Lucius feigning not to be impressed, would please Thor fine.

Chapter Three

Lexa moaned as she drifted back to consciousness. Her shoulder ached and pleaded with her not to move it. Warmth from a crackling fire bathed her side, and was a comforting offset compared to the chill on her back from the stone slab she laid upon. A cave of sandstone carved smooth to a point at its roof with a hole left open for smoke to escape from revealed itself above her.

The queasy feeling in her stomach when she tried to sit up made her wonder just what hit her. She laid back down, her head throbbing. One touch to her scalp found something caked and matted in her hair. Scraping it beneath her nails her fingertips were stained dark red; dried blood.

"Was beginning to think you weren't going to pull through, Sister."

The familiar voice of Sorsha allowed Lexa to take a deep breath, they'd survived the battle with the Atlantean sorcerer, Xanatos. "Did we win?" she croaked. Her throat was dry, parched.

"In a manner of speaking."

Lexa flinched as a waterskin plopped onto her stomach.

"Where are we?" Lexa groaned, rolling to her side. She took a pull, quenching her thirst. Her stomach grumbled from the smell of meat cooking. A pig lay on a spit over the fire, filling the room with that smell only pig meat can make. She hadn't eaten in a while.

"On our way to Cap Canna, should reach it tomorrow."

"Cap Canna? Thought there was only desert between Cherteri and Cap Canna. Nothing that would support…this." Lexa motioned the waterskin toward the ceiling of the tiny room.

"I changed that."

Confused at Sorsha's response, Lexa craned her neck, wincing as she moved, to address Sorsha behind her. "What do you mean you—"

Sorsha was donned in purple lace dress so intricate she ought to be a queen sitting on a throne, not a chair carved from the rock wall. A far stretch from her brushed steel battle armour bearing the crest of the Raven. Her once curly crimson locks were now black as night, straight as an arrow, and framing a face of cold indifference. She looked like a completely different woman than the one Lexa had come to know, not just in her physical attire, but in the way she sat, carried herself, and stared back at her. Lexa took pride in her skills at noticing fine details, it aided her in her trade as a thief, but as hard as she tried, only the voice of the woman beside her was familiar. There wasn't a trace left of the Sorsha she'd known.

"Wow." Lexa spoke plainly after a moment of taking in Sorsha's appearance, almost regretted it, but knew Sorsha would take no offence. "How long was I out?" Lexa sat up, rubbing her shoulder.

"You don't approve?" Sorsha tilted her head, glared as if into Lexa's very soul.

"Just surprised to see you out of your armor. Last I can remember we were fighting for our lives." Lexa ran her fingers through her hair, plucking caked blood free in clumps. "I'm sure there isn't a man alive that wouldn't come calling." Lexa mused, but with caution. Sorsha had a way about her that gave levity to any situation involving men. Especially how she'd reveled in teasing them with her wares only to leave them wanting. But with such a drastic change in Sorsha, not just her appearance but…everything, Lexa held back.

"They don't interest me." Sorsha said coldly, and stared up at the ceiling.

"Who?"

"Men. None living anyways, they can all burn as far as I'm concerned."

"None living?" Lexa glanced around the tiny stone hut; they were alone. "What of the others? What of—"

"Dead."

Lexa's throat dried, made it hard to swallow.

"Dead, no, all of them. Even—" The name couldn't slip past Lexa's lips, Eric.

"They're dead. All of them. Soon the rest will follow. Now eat, you need to keep up your strength, Sister." Sorsha stared at the grease sizzling into the fire from the pig roasting on a spit above its flames."

"How…I mean?" She wanted to ask about Eric, the thief that first infuriated her, the man that had won her heart. All conversation had left Lexa's mind, only one question remained, how? "We had the upper hand." It was likely, but she didn't want to accept that her and Sorsha were the only ones left. "Eric." She covered her mouth, pressing her fingers hard against her lips. Tears welled, but she wouldn't let one fall. Eric was a formidable opponent, fast, strong, cunning, and that's without considering his wolf side. "And Thor?" How could he have fallen too? More a barbarian than anything, he was a force of his own, and surprisingly had more than just brute strength but wits as well.

But when it came to wits no other bested Lucius. Lexa wasn't the only one who lost somebody. Lucius had warmed Sorsha's cold heart toward men. Sorsha's days with Lucius, just like her days with Eric, had been brief, but both of them had taken more than a liking to them. Sorsha had all but vowed to be with Lucius and no other. "Oh Sorsha, Lucius. I'm so sorry. I—"

"Raven." Sorsha stared deeper into the fire, leaning closer.

"What?" Why was she insisting she be called by her chosen mercenary name?

Sorsha remained stiff, but her eyes widened, darted to lock with Lexa's. Sorsha repeated herself, shortly, "Raven." Her gaze locked on Lexa's trailed for a moment, then shifted back to a target in the flames. Lexa caught the fire light flicker off of something just above Sorsha's left breast, partially revealed due to the plunging neckline of her dress.

Embedded in Sorsha's chest, was a piece of Xanatos' stone of power.

Lexa let out a slow, controlled breath, as if she was about to steal something valuable and was surrounded by city guards. But where she sat now was far more dangerous. From this moment on, she would require cunning, guile, and deception; all of which Lexa was a master of.

They weren't sisters, yet Sorsha referred to her as one. She'd never done that before. The icy glare from her blue eyes was nothing new, but it was as if there was a lack of something in them. Not determination, Sorsha had plenty of that creating her persona of the Raven to lead mercenaries to plunder the corrupt and wealthy, and keep her true identity secret from the world. But there was more to her now, more and less. The shard of the gem. It did something to Sorsha, changed her. More bitterness, sharpness, and distain for men—if that was even possible. But there was less...kinship in her words and her tone, less...compassion.

"Hello?" Before Lexa could say another word, a voice from outside the cave called out. A voice she was sure would be softer had its owner not been traveling in the desert. "Hello?" Came the voice again, this time the words spoken became more discernible.

"Enter, Sister," replied Raven.

A beautiful round face dusted with the desert and framed with long dark hair joined them in the firelight through the entrance's burlap flap. The woman paused and swept over the tiny cave, Lexa, and Sorsha, with her large brown eyes. A smile grew on the woman's face, and she stepped inside. "Well, this certainly wasn't what I was expecting to find on the caravan route, but I sure am happy I did." She shook her cloak, letting the desert puff from it. "A pair of women in the only thing other than sand for as far as the eye can see. Name's Darla, and...if I'm not mistaken...I think we've met," Darla said to Raven. "At a tavern in Cherteri a few nights back—the Feisty Goat."

"I remember."

Darla took a deep whiff of the succulent pig's aroma. "I have to thank you; I don't normally take payment for bedding a man. But that was no man you gave me gold for. By rights, *I* should have paid *you* for introducing me to Thor. I would have bedded him without the gold, but a woman has to take her coin when she can get it."

"You know Thor?" Lexa asked, restraining herself from glancing at Raven. Sorsha had no love for the man, and little tolerance. What the Raven might do to Darla for the sheer mention of his name was unpredictable, especially being under the influence of an Atlantean curse. Would Raven slay this wayward woman where she stands? If so, Lexa sifted through her options. What move to make, if any? What words would set the Raven's wrath upon her? Stretching her shoulder, Lexa knew her chances of surviving a fight with Sorsha would test her every skill, and going to war with her friend was something she hoped to avoid.

Darla looked at the ceiling and sighed. "A woman could settle down with that one, if he could be tamed. Wish he was with us when we left Cherteri."

"Us?" Lexa looked past Darla to the cave's entrance.

"There was four of us that left Cherteri, now I'm all that's left." Darla shifted her tone, sat on the floor, warmed her hands by the fire. "Friends since we were little girls. Cut down by a band of thieves. Not like we had much to take anyways, barely saved up enough to start over in Cap Canna as a group." A tear ran down her cheek, carving a line through the fine film of dirt the desert left on her. Wiping it aside she continued. "Honourless cowards, attacking women."

Bandits were one thing, but thieves they were not. Herself and Eric happened upon each other trying to raid the King's coffers, but it wasn't until Lexa met Lucius that they succeeded in making away with more than they could carry on their backs. Lexa prided herself on being a master at her trade, with a code that went along with it. Sorsha, Eric, Lucius, and even Thor shared that code. "They weren't thieves, thieves have honour and take from those who can afford it, they were—"

"Pigs," Raven said, cutting off Lexa. "You're safe now, Darla. I'll never let *any* man harm you again."

Darla huffed. "I'm no fighter. If I was, maybe they'd still be alive. Maybe if I'd tried harder to bring Thor with me he could have saved them."

"You need no man." Raven stood from her stone chair, glaring down at Darla. "I can make you better, make you a warrior. Make you never need to rely on a man again."

With those words, Lexa had her suspicions confirmed about Xanatos' stone effecting her friend. Sorsha always had a distaste for men, that was no secret. But the sheer hatred she displayed now, and calling herself Raven. Sure, it was her alias as she ran the most feared group of mercenaries the land had known, but she only stressed it in her force's company. It was as if she wanted all men dead. Lucius's death, Lexa decided, that's what pushed Sorsha over the edge, coupled with the stone in her chest, there's no telling what was going on in her head.

"How?" asked Darla. She had a timid nature she'd probably carried with her for her entire life.

"Like this." Raven, not letting Darla squeak out another word, moved faster than Lexa had ever seen Sorsha move. She rounded the fire, took hold of Darla's neck in one hand, and hoisted her clear off the floor. Darla clawed at Raven's wrist. Before Lexa could stand, or even shout for her to stop, Raven slammed her palm on Darla's forehead, grasping her head.

The tiny cave lit up.

Crimson light escaped from both the shard in Raven's chest and her palm on Darla's forehead.

Lexa raised her hand to shade her eyes, but the flash vanished as fast as it appeared, leaving crimson spots lingering in Lexa's vision.

Darla collapsed to the cave floor.

Raven walked around the fire as if nothing had happened and cut a strip of meat from the pig, and draped it over the end of the spit out of the fires reach. "Eat." She commanded.

Lexa wasn't sure who Raven was talking to, her or Darla. But Darla was the first of them to move. She touched her forehead, rubbing it. "What have you done?" She asked Raven, with a steady voice that sounded nothing like the timid girl who'd walked into the cave.

Raven's answer was to whirl around with the blade in her hand—plunging it at Darla's throat.

Darla rose to her feet, and in one fluid motion side-stepped the attack, slapped the blade free from Raven's grasp, took hold of it with her other hand and thrust it at Raven's ribs.

Lexa pushed herself up, drew her blade, and watched the once timid girl move just as she'd seen Sorsha move during battle, with skill and confidence.

Raven side-stepped in turn, grasped Darla's wrist and twirled her around.

Raven's violet lace whirled, as did Darla's brown robes, both flaring out as their dance ended with Raven behind Darla, and her blade pressed against Darla's throat.

"That's how," Raven said, pausing for a moment, then releasing Darla and shoving her forward.

Darla caught her balance, stood stiff, glaring at Raven; a look Lexa had seen numerous times before on her friend.

"You now have *my* skills, Sister. A piece of me…so to say." Raven sat back in her chair.

Darla's temper cooled as her glare eased. She stared at her fists, unfurled her fingers, and after a deep breath she replied. "Thank you. I understand now. What I've been lacking. No more"—Darla paused, looking up as if in deep thought—"never again shall I be a man's prey." She plucked the strip of pig Raven had draped over the spit, bit a piece off, and with a full mouth grunted. "Or merely one of their playthings."

Lexa sat on the slab, setting her blade beside her to be brandished should the need arise. Darla had obtained battle skills like Sorsha, but Sorsha's distaste for men as well. Weighing her options, as she always did, Lexa chose her next words carefully. "So, what's the plan? You've never been lacking of a good one, Raven."

Raven smiled. "We eat, keep up our strength, then head for Cap Canna where I shall liberate our sisters and carve out my kingdom. As sorceress supreme, the first woman ever to wield the power of Atlantis." Raven paused, sat up straight. "Now eat up, Sisters. We've a lengthy journey ahead of us."

Despite the rumble in her belly, Lexa had lost her apatite. "I'm strong enough on my own without the pig, besides, I've heard Cap Canna has the richest of fruits. And I'm not certain I can keep anything down just yet." In truth, Lexa wasn't sure she wanted to trust where Sorsha had gotten the pig from, it's not as if there were herds of swine roaming the desert. "As for your newfound power, I hope you'll use it to benefit all the women of that coastal city."

"Not just them, the women of the world shall be free from those gawking knuckle draggers that think only with their loins...pigs. And with you by my side as my second, the skilled master thief that you are, we shall be unstoppable. I'd almost say your as deadly as I am with those blades of yours...almost."

"*Almost?*" Lexa grinned, prompting a laugh from Raven, something the two of them found so easy to do when Raven was still Sorsha. Lexa's grin was not solely in response to Raven's jest, though. She'd confirmed her place at Raven's side. A place that may allow her, if she played the game of deception right, to rip Xanatos' stone from Raven's chest, and if her fortunes held, return Sorsha to the mercenary leader she once was. It stood to reason separating her friend from that cursed Atlantean shard would revert Sorsha back to her former self.

The key to this heist would be waiting for the moment to present itself, and if it did not, Lexa would create such a moment. She laid back on the slab, silently sliding her dagger out of site beside her thigh, keeping it hidden yet at the ready. She closed her eyes listening to every motion made by the other two women, and scrutinized their conversation until they settled in for the night. Aside from the difference in voice, and the domineering chain of command, Darla could have been mistaken for Raven due to her wording, her tone, her immediate agreement with whatever Raven proclaimed.

Lexa was thorough, always had been, when planning a heist. Dealing with sorcery was uncharted territory. There were so many variables to consider, and she wouldn't make a play until she resolved them or at the least had a back-up plan should her original fail. One thing was certain, she wished her fallen companions were at her side to lend their aid, and advice. So, she settled for the only option left, recalling every conversation regarding the amulet, Atlantis, and Xanatos, that she had with her fallen companions. Would separating the amulet shard from Raven release Sorsha? Or would she have to destroy the shard? What *would* destroy the Atlantean shard? Fire? Grinding it to dust? Submerging it in liquid metal? Could *she* touch the stone to remove it without being compromised herself? Would Darla be released from Xanatos' curse if her efforts proved successful? Hoping a good night's rest would bring answers to the questions she mulled over; Lexa released them from her mind and allowed herself to mourn her fallen friends. Tears ran freely, streaking her temples. Her last thoughts before drifting off settled on her love, Eric, and their final embrace before she lost him.

Chapter Four

Thor grinned as Lucius hauled up a cask of wine from the belly of the ship, and two cups. "There is not enough in this barrel to quench my thirst after that jaunt. I should be exhausted, but I'm not." Lucius said, setting his cargo on a table by the ship's wheel. "I haven't slept since the mountain came down and nearly crushed me. Must be whatever Xanatos did. Up there I was compelled to do as he said." He uncorked the cask and filled the polished copper cups. "That feeling went away when Sorsha killed him, but it came back the next morning. I had to get to the Red Ox. As if *he* ordered me to do so." Lucius handed a cup to Thor, resting an elbow between the wooden toggles of the wheel. "As soon as my feet made the Red Ox, rather it's remnants, it was as if a primal urge to make it there was gone, and I was free once more. Like I could go about my business. Yet I know there is something missing, something he took. My passion, my spirit, my desires. I feel…empty."

"Like the Raven's mercenaries, he did to you what he did to them. Turned them into a slave that must due his bidding," Thor said, not holding back.

"Straight to the point. That's why I keep you around. But I am pretty sure a dead man, Atlantean sorcerer or not, can't order me around once he's passed. That doesn't explain why I had to go to my favorite tavern, or what's left of it. What *did* happen to it, you get in a brawl about paying Old Red or something?"

Thor looked back at Cherteri over the deck's rail. "No, she did that all by herself." He nodded at the city.

Lucius followed his nod and squinted. The moment Lucius caught sight of the crimson fog furling within the city's wall was obvious to Thor. His one-time cell mate, the great planner, was wrought with confusion, furrowing his brow.

"She? She who? Atlantis only let men wield the mystic arts, and the Last Atlantean is dead. So, who—"

"Sorsha"—Thor locked his gaze on Lucius—"Sorsha now commands you."

Lucius paused, shaking his head, pondering Thor's words.

"What am I missing?"

Thor studied Lucius: his face was pale, a mix of concern, panic, and anger. The only way to tell him was exact and to the point, the only way he knew how. "There's a piece of Xanatos's gem buried in her flesh." Thor touched his chest indicating where.

"She's not herself, she did this." He held out his hand toward Cherteri. "Calls herself the Raven, changed her garb, her hair, her very self before my eyes. Changed by sorcery. She flew away on her winged horse with Lexa still knocked out. Then flattened the tavern with me in it, but not before saying she wished you were there, at the Ox, at the very spot you ceased your journey from the mountain." From the way Lucius's eyes darted from the deck boards to the city and then to the mountain, Thor could see Lucius was having trouble processing what he'd said, or at the least having trouble accepting it. "There's a part of him in her now, a part of Xanatos. Fueling her rage. I was loading up to go in search of her when you showed up."

"That's why our course is Tenzin," Lucius said more to himself than to Thor.

"Best guess is she's gone south. It's the path where her mercenaries once camped out. It's familiar to her. As good a place to start as any, seeing as how she's on that winged horse and can't be tracked. The wind is in our favor." Thor strode from the wheel, tugged at the ship's rigging, unfurling a sail. "Should help us catch up."

"Tenzin," Lucius said.

Repeating Thor's words was something Thor had not known Lucius to do. He was an intelligent man, devising Cherteri's defenses against Xanatos, constructing the ship they stood upon, and successfully empty the King's coffers, but he was never one to ponder something as if he could not contemplate it.

Thor decided to break the silence, and Lucius's internal struggle, by jesting with him. Something he was as good at as he was with his blade. He could, and had infuriated Sorsha to no end, yet turned her, convinced her to see that which he wanted. And she was one of the strongest-willed people Thor had met in all his travels. His way was that of a warrior, a sword for hire, but one with wits as well. Wits that he would use to ease his companion's troubled mind. "How'd you really get free of Xanatos's lair? Rabbit hole you say. I doubt there was a cavern large enough for your enlarged head."

Lucius, taking a moment to shift back to the man Thor knew him to be, grinned. "Trade secrets my friend, just like devising our escape from the barracks. I've always got a plan."

"No, no, no. Taking credit for our escape. Your irons still had you chained to the floor while I walked around freely. You can't just—"

Lucius picked up Thor by the base of his breastplate with one hand, and held him over his head with ease. "I can."

"Whoa." Lucius was a head shorter than Thor, and though he was well-built he couldn't match Thor's strength. He grasped Lucius' shoulder and wrist; both were hard as pieces of wood. He was at the smaller man's mercy unless Thor pulled a blade.

"Whoa is right." Lucius put Thor down, unharmed. "Seems I'm stronger than you now. Helped to dig my way out of that rubble. Besides, only half the mountain collapsed, not all of it. Thought you warrior types noticed the details in things." Lucius smirked.

"Oh, we do, just like how I noticed you're not nearly as strong as me. I was...ah...just playing along with your demonstration. Recall I've got such a keen eye that I even found your stash of wine."

"Congratulations. You found the only ship in the harbor, with my gold, and rummaged around long enough to decipher the difference between a cask of wine and one filled with grain. Your skills never cease to amaze me."

Thor punched Lucius on the shoulder. "It's good to have you back."

"That's all you got?" Lucius rubbed his shoulder.

"Oh, I've got a lot more, just not sure you can handle it."

Lucius chuckled. "Let's be on our way. You *did* figure out how to re-engage the rudder, I assume."

"I was just about to get to that. But since you're here, why don't you take care of that while I tend to the rest of the sails."

"Then you can tell me what became of Eric, you haven't said a word about him yet."

As if to answer Lucius's question, the howl of a wolf filled the air as the final rays of the sun dropped below the horizon. Thor peered in the direction, contemplating how he might contain his cousin if he failed to turn him from his wolf form into a man. He'd failed in his attempt to do so in the past; Lexa was the one who broke through the enraged beast's blood drunk rage enough to calm Eric down, and let him revert back to his normal self. Battling his cousin to the death was not an adventure he wanted to be part of. He drained his cup of Lucius' sweet wine, glaring at the foothills across the river.

Chapter Five

Lexa woke to the sun's early rays shining through the cave's entrance. Rotating her shoulder to ease its stiffness, she saw Raven and Darla still slumbering on stone slabs that she was sure had not been there last night. Moving with the skills she'd honed over the years as a thief, she left the cave without making a sound.

The tiny cave was located in the very center of the caravan route, made of a solid slab of smooth brown stone. She'd never traveled to Cap Canna, those that built the caravan route so long ago would not have done it with this out-of-place structure in its center, of that, she was sure. Tethered to a stone rail beside the cave were two horses, and one bearing wings, the same one Sorsha had taken to the mountain for their siege against the Last Atlantean.

"Ready to set out," Raven said, exiting the cave.

Lexa did her best not to show she'd been startled. Someone sneaking up on her was something not easily accomplished. "You know me, always ready. Though I'm not sure how you got me to the middle of the desert, you must have tied me to my mount so I didn't fall to the sand." She craned her neck, prying casually to find out what actually happened.

"I have my ways. Now that we're no longer airborne, it'll take longer to reach Cap Canna. It's best we saddle up. Darla." Raven commanded over her shoulder. "Get up."

Now that we're not airborne? What did Raven mean by *we*? Only one horse had wings. Lexa doubted she could have been stabilized enough to fly while being unconscious. She'd seen how the winged horses move, bounding in the sky as they soared, nothing similar to the smooth motion of a bird. The other two horses, without wings, were as different in appearance as Sorsha was from Raven. One was packed with what she'd expect a tavern maid to burden a mount with. Bundles of clothing, silk and lace, rolled and tied neatly in place, along with a single waterskin hung on one horse. The other looked more like that of a mount a desert nomad would ride. One laden with waterskins, sacks of dried dusty leather, what looked like a collapsible tent, and a cookpot. Certainly, not a mount procured in Cherteri. Perhaps on the way she could get Raven to reveal more about what exactly happened since their battle with the last Atlantean. As for now, Lexa mounted up, choosing the nomad-looking horse. "If we're still that far out it's good you found us this one. Looks as if it's used to surviving this harsh condition better than Darla's." Lexa ran her fingers through the horses' dusty mane, gauging Raven's face, waiting to see if she would say how she procured the animal. When she didn't, Lexa turned her horse east toward Cap Canna. "Let's get going, I'm getting hungry."

Darla came out of the cave rubbing the sleep from her eyes, adjusting them to the morning sun. "There's plenty of pig left, shouldn't we eat before heading out?

"There's plenty of pigs in Cap Canna," Raven said. "Saddle up."

That confirmed it for Lexa. Raven said nothing as to her chosen mount, nor did Darla as she emerged from the cave. Something was amiss, something about how she got to this spot with Raven in the middle of the desert. Normally, when dealing with Sorsha, the direct approach was the best course of action. But with Raven...Lexa thought it best to use her guile and cunning to pry information from her nearly unrecognizable friend.

Darla made for her mount, but stopped short, her shifting gaze searching the rolling dunes for something. She dropped to the sand, buried her hands beneath its grains. "Did you feel that?"

"What?" Lexa asked.

"Very good, sister. Seems I passed more of...myself onto you than I intended to." Sorsha traced her fingers over the shard embedded in her chest. "I'll have to be more wary with our next sister."

Darla closed her eyes, and mumbled something in a tongue Lexa could not make out. A flash of crimson surged beneath her palm then rippled through the sand at a good pace in every direction.

"Much more wary," Sorsha said, raising her brow at what Darla had done. "You can feel it, yes?"

Darla nodded her response.

"You shall sit well by my side. The only sister to bear...a grander portion of my gifts."

"We have to hurry, Raven." Darla stood and climbed atop her horse without pause as if she understood what Raven knew, what was yet to be revealed to Lexa.

"I know, sister, I know. Our journey awaits."

"What am I missing out on? What's the hurry, other than putting this desert to our backside?" Lexa glanced at the sky shading her eyes with her palm from the rising sun. She wanted to press the matter, digging for answers was her nature. It was rare she ever made a move without first gathering as much information as possible. But with what just transpired, and these women before her, put an air of caution to her words choosing to focus on their banter rather than their sorcery. The last thing she wanted was to have Raven alter her wits. She would need all she has to free Sorsha from Raven's clutches.

"The world will be forever changed. The destruction of Atlantis saw to that." Raven replied, her gaze locked on Lexa. "A minor oversight." She grinned, maliciously. "But turns out it was needed, to reveal my Kingdom."

It seemed like Raven was speaking more to herself rather than answering her question, a mannerism Lexa had not seen before in Sorsha.

Darla nodded her agreement. Both women acting as if there was no more to be said of the matter, as if they clarified their need for haste, instead they filled Lexa's head with more questions. The most pressing of which circled Darla. If Darla has Raven's power, Xanatos' power, then that complicates things. One sorceress would be difficult enough to handle, let alone two. How is she to deal with Darla? If she strips the gem from Raven, and that turns Sorsha back to normal, will Darla loose whatever *gifts* Raven has bestowed upon her? Her gut told her Raven was not to be trusted, Sorsha yes, but not Raven. Thus, she would wait, and try to gently pry the answers she sought on their way to Cap Canna.

"Well then, our let's be on our way. The sooner we get there the better. I never was one for sand and sun, unless there's an ocean's waves lapping my feet." Lexa kicked her mount forward and led them east.

"Atta girl," said Raven. "Always at the ready."

Lexa didn't reply, she just pressed her mount forward, wanting to distance herself from the never-ending curse of Atlantis's power. Their journey she planned to use well, to contemplate what the women at her back spoke so cryptic of.

~*~

The desert gave way to small thorny shrubs that became larger the further they traveled. Eventually, the shrubs gave way to patches of brown grass, followed by lush shrubbery surrounding the caravan route that itself had shifted from marked sand to hard-packed dirt.

They had traveled most of the day, and those final words between her and Raven outside the cave were the last they had spoken to each other the entire trip. Making the day in the blistering sun seem longer than it should. A few words between her and Darla was all that Lexa had for conversation. Darla's mindset was identical to Sorsha's, or Raven's, so much so it made Lexa want to gallop off on her own to be rid of whatever sorcery Raven had bestowed upon Darla, wanting no part of it herself. Lexa decided silent travel was the best way to go, following suit with the other woman's examples. Raven rode behind them both, overseeing them. Lexa felt Raven's gaze on her back, like that of a true Atlantean, a true slaver. Her travels with Sorsha had been brief, yet they were filled with jests, contemplations, tactics, and talk of their men. With every passing turn of the glass Lexa's fear grew, fear that her friend had become truly lost to the control of the sorcerous gem, and all it stood for.

The smell of fresh water made Lexa sit up straighter, crane her neck. "We're close."

"No. We're here." Raven held up her palm as they crested a hill bringing Cap Canna into view. "Cap Canna, the coastal paradise cut off from the world by the vast desert."

Raven did not misspeak; the rumors were true. The lands appearance matched the tales Lexa had heard. Cap Canna looked like a paradise. Cresting the hill revealed a lush plateau dipping before her, full of trees weighted with orange, green, and red fruit, all supported by canals dug from a winding river cascading through heavily treed hills beyond the orchards. A single stone road presented itself, winding its way through the plateau, then carved a path out of steep cliffs at the plateau's edge leading down to a land-bridge connecting the island city to the rest of the world. With a population far less than half that of Cherteri, and protected by the natural barrier of the bay, it stood with not a wall in sight.

The river spilled down rocky cliffs to the bay of sea water surrounding the city. Mist from the waterfall glistened on Lexa's skin as they traversed the winding road; a refreshing change from the harsh desert air, Lexa pulled its fragrance deeper into her chest, tasting its rich life-giving essence.

It wasn't until they reached the land-bridge that Lexa took in the full beauty of the city. Looking back, the spray from the waterfall seemed to create an ever-moving rainbow she hadn't noticed when moving through it. The city itself gave off a warm inviting feeling. No gate, no guards; just a kindly looking woman with long gray hair lounging on the shoreline beside a warning bell large enough she could fit inside it. It stood as the only sign of preparation against attack. A far cry from Cherteri with its overwhelming defenses behind its high walls designed by Lucius.

Lexa nodded at the old woman. The woman nodded back, accompanied by a toothless smile. A smile that hardened the moment she set eyes on Raven's winged mount. Before a word could be spoken, or the warning bell could be struck, Raven leapt from her mount and slapped her palm on the old woman's forehead; just as she'd done to Darla in the cave.

Lexa froze, wanting to cry out for Raven to stop, but held her tongue knowing winning the battle to spare this woman would not be the tipping point for Lexa to win the war she alone was fighting.

"Who's in charge here?" asked Raven of the old woman.

"You are, my lady." Replied the old woman; not a streak of kindness left across her face.

Raven nodded and continued forward.

"That's what she's doing," Lexa said under her breath.

Her words were not as silent as she'd thought, for without warning, or looking back at her, Raven asked. "What is it that I'm doing?"

"Xanatos took your men from you, you're replenishing your ranks," replied Lexa, panicking, yet coming up with something so as to not bring the wrath of the Raven down upon her.

"You're half right, I'm building an army of warriors. One not made up of cutthroats and mercenaries that only think with their loins. One made entirely of highly skilled women." Raven turned to Lexa, and with a grin, added, "Your idea."

"My idea?"

"Yes, yours." Raven winked. "On the way to the mountain. Or did you forget your imparted wisdom? You said next time I should be more choosey about the company I keep, or something like that. As my most trusted advisor, and friend, I've taken your words to heart."

Two things about what Raven said ran through Lexa's mind. She'd somehow raised herself in Raven's ranks from a past memory of Sorsha's to become not only her second but now her trusted advisor. As for Raven's heart, Lexa wasn't sure there was one left in the woman before her.

"That's why we work so well together," Lexa said, attempting to keep up appearances. "We've gone through some grand adventures, you and me."

"It'll be easier now, this I assure you," Raven added as a burly man approached her.

"Well, what do we have here, a tavern maid in need of a night's pay? Three for the price of one?" The man licked his lips looking Raven up and down.

"This time, there won't be any of them." Raven pointed a thumb at the burly man as she spoke to Lexa. Turning around, she strode toward him swaying her hips seductively, and raised her hand. "No pigs."

A thin violet tendril shot out from her finger, hit the burly man in the chest, and spread over his body. The violet shape of the man shrank and contorted, then dropped to the ground. The tendril faded away, disappeared. Raven let her hand fall to her side, raised her chin, and strutted past a brown haired pig with black spots emerging from its violet cocoon.

"Your true form looks better on you." She kicked the pig, who scurried away. She then turned her attention to a gathering crowd, raised her palm, and sent a blend of violet tendrils and crimson beams weaving among the bystanders. The violet tendrils engulfed each man, the exact same way as the one Raven had just turned into a pig. The crimson beams struck each woman on the forehead, the same as what happened to Darla.

Lexa's breath caught at the sight before her. The horse she sat upon, the pig in the cave, the only pig in the entire desert that Raven had just happened upon. Raven had transformed the horse's owner, some unsuspecting man, into an animal. Lexa was more relieved than thankful that she hadn't joined in on the feast the night before.

Chapter Six

"How much longer you figure it'll take?" Thor asked Lucius, leaning against the steering wheel of the ship.

"Seven days ride. Three by ship sounds right. Though I've never been to Tenzin. You?" Lucius replied, lounging in a hammock he'd strung from the mast to the rail.

"Once."

"And?"

"Let's just say that no man will ever be lonely in Tenzin." Thor grinned. "It's a town of a thousand good times and a thousand good people. Nearly everyone's tied to the fishing of the river in one way or another. The merchant's, tavern maids, traders, even the few surrounding farmers. The river's so bountiful the entire town is well fed and cares only for their nightly drink and dicing."

"Sounds like your kind of place."

"*Our* kind of place." Thor corrected Lucius. "It's a place like no other. More a sprawling city of taverns and inns than that of your typical city. Has a feel to it, like all are welcome. And all are, as long as their purse is full. Wine, and I mean stuff to meat even your high standards, costs coppers not silvers. You'll see. I had to be wary last time. Inexpensive wine, and plenty of it, can make for poor decision making and far too much dicing."

"Left with an empty purse did you?" Lucius chuckled. "Couldn't handle your wine?"

"Let's just say Tenzin has a reputation for giving a man *hope* of winning a fortune. But I suspect most do not let on how much their purse has been emptied. With all the gold we hold, and the fact that there's no king. We'll be running the place in no time. That's if Sorsha hasn't laid waste to the place due to someone offering her a wine not up to her liking."

"She wouldn't do that. Sure, she's strong-willed, but she's not unreasonable. And if she does lay waste to anyone, it would be you. Leaving me alone at the mountain like that, infuriating her to no end as only you can do. And then trying to make away with my gold to boot." Lucius pulled the brim of his cap down over his eyes. "I think I just might distance myself from you when we find her. Don't want any accidental backlash aimed at your head hitting mine."

"Our wager was that *you* entertain *me*, not the other way around." Thor tossed a jug of wine into Lucius's gut, causing him to fall from his hammock as he attempted to salvage the contents.

"I'll still win that wager. But even though I brought a wagon full of wine with us there's no need to waist it." Lucius pulled at his soiled shirt.

"Figured that was the only way to shut you up. You may not have realized my friend, but your tongue has become nearly as forked as the woman we're chasing."

"You mistake a forked tongue for witty banter, which you obviously can't keep up with." Lucius tossed the cracked jug over the railing, after which he stood motionless looking toward the western shore. "You…want to see this."

Lucius's tone put speed to Thor's legs as he crossed the deck and followed Lucius's gaze. It wasn't hard to spot what grabbed Lucius's attention. "Drop the anchor."

Eric was standing on the river bank, naked as the day he was born save for a thin cotton belt around his waist.

~*~

"Good to see you, old friend." Lucius tossed a rope to Eric wading into the river toward the ship, then pulled Eric up from the water to the deck.

"You two, on this ship, heading my direction, was the last thing I expected to see." Eric took the robe Thor had scrounged up from below deck.

"I'm just happy you're not furry anymore, cousin," Thor said, waiting for Eric to don the robe and cover himself before giving him a pat on the shoulder. "Wasn't sure how we'd find you. Especially after how you took off from the mountain."

"It took a few nights to come to my senses, that much I can admit." Eric adjusted the ill-fitting robe, stretching it to fit his shoulders, flexing his arms. "The rest is still somewhat blurry."

"What do you remember?" Lucius handed Eric a jug of wine.

Eric took a long drink then dropped down to the deck and placed the jug beside him. "Lexa. I remember her clear as a wineless day. Then I get flashes of Xanatos, that winged wolf that did this to me, the forest, a caravan, foothills, and then the river. It's not much, just flashes. I know I sat at the river for more than a few turns of the glass. That's where I…woke up. Couldn't decide which way to go, north or south, I really had no idea how far I'd traveled. Or for how long." He took another swig and nodded to Lucius. "Better than the stuff you kept in your boot."

"Yeah, I outfitted the ship from my sanctuary. Good thing I came along before Thor here compromised the stash," replied Lucius.

"He would drink it dry on us."

"Wouldn't put it past him."

"You need to eat." Thor threw a loaf of bread at his cousin. "And you need to curb what you consider witty banter," Thor said to Lucius. Taking the jug from Eric, Thor drank deep as well and looked out over the river bank. "Lexa's alive."

"What!" Eric jumped to his feet. "I saw her, the blood, was sure she was…"

"Nope." Thor shook his head. "Got her back to Cherteri myself."

"Where is she now?"

"With Sorsha, we're tracking them down, hoping they headed south."

"What do you mean hoping?" asked Eric. "How come you don't know if you were with them? What happened at the mountain? Is Xanatos dead?"

Eric's barrage of questions prompted Lucius to step in, put a hand on Thor's shoulder and pull the jug of wine free from Thor's grasp. "You're not very good at telling tales, are you?" Lucius asked of Thor without expecting a response. He turned to Eric, gave him the jug. "I'll talk, you drink. The great communicator over here." Lucius pointed his thumb at Thor. "Can fill in anything I've left out."

Thor shook his head and went below to get his own jug of wine while Lucius got Eric up to speed. Thor returned, and when Lucius finished, he handed Lucius the jug and asked Eric, "Any questions?"

Eric's eyes searched the deck as if a question was scribed on to it. "He's right, you're not good at telling stories, cousin."

"This coming from a guy that stands nude on a riverbank." Thor chuckled. "I may not be the best at stories, but I know how to track. Been following your howls for three days now. Knew we'd pick you up eventually. You're welcome." Thor slapped Eric on the back as he stepped beside him to lean out over the deck rail.

"Actually…those howls weren't mine."

Thor and Lucius locked eyes with one another. "Come again?" asked Lucius.

"Great." Thor threw his arm in the air, and his jug into the river. "Like we didn't have enough problems, now we've gotta deal with more of Xanatos's wolves."

"Least we know they can't make any more of them from their bites. When they're gone, the land will be free of them for good." Lucius raised his jug to take a drink.

"Actually…" Eric trailed off.

"What. What now?" Thor scowled, eyeing his cousin. "Xanatos' cursed wolves couldn't change anyone through a bite, and he isn't making any more of them. Don't tell me you bit more people? Made wolves that can make more wolves?" Thor held his palms out toward the land. "There isn't even anybody out here to bite. Unless you mated with a pack of wild dogs. How could—"

"A caravan?" guessed Lucius, interrupting Thor.

"A caravan," Eric agreed. "At least I think so…from what I can remember. Like I said, it's kinda foggy remembering what happened when I'm…different."

"I know I've said I'm always up for a good adventure." Thor clenched his fist. "But this is getting ridiculous. We're right back where we started when I got to Cherteri. Even dealing with a sorcerer again…or sorceress…Sorsha." Thor pounded his fist on the rail.

"We did come out on top last time. If you don't count Sorsha being possessed, and you running off into the woods." Lucius nodded to Eric. "And me losing…whatever he took from me. We're still alive."

"I need a drink." Thor turned toward the galley doors.

"You may wanna hold off on that." Lucius's tone suggested something was awry. The cousins both looked to Lucius, then to the sky he was staring at, and the black cloud overtaking it. "I think we're getting closer to Tenzin. The only thing that could make a plume like that would be a city with an unchecked blaze."

Chapter Seven

After two days in Cap Canna, Lexa found herself in the midst of an army. Everywhere she turned another woman bearing Sorsha's temperament appeared to either salute her, or call her Lady Lexa. She knew she'd missed her chance in the cave to free Sorsha from Xanatos's gem and leave Raven as nothing more than a bad dream.

Lexa was never alone, nor was Raven; her army of three or four-hundred made sure to that. Even walking the streets had been cumbersome due to the equal number of pigs running wild. Not a man was left in human form on the paradise island known as Cap Canna. Every man had been transformed to a hairy pig with varying colored spots. Now, Lexa was hoping Raven would see her mistake in transforming the men to pigs; or at least smell her mistake. Lexa found herself, and Raven's army, moving to higher ground due to wrinkling their noses at the pungent smell of half a city full of swine.

"We need to talk." Lexa said to Raven as she strode into what was once a great hall where the king of Cap Canna would celebrate the annual harvest. Being more of a farmer than a king, the people loved him. He over-saw the island without tax, but with delegation to keep all happy, well-fed, their bellies full of wine, and the city in good trading standard with other kingdoms. Now, the hall had been turned into Raven's war room. Its tables were covered with every map the city had to offer. Half a dozen of Raven's army were present at all times. "I said we need to talk."

"I heard you the first time," said Raven, running her finger along a map littered with tiny wooden figurines of ships and soldiers. "No need to get testy."

I'm the only one who can, thought Lexa. The rest of these women are shells of their former selves, and if I don't play the game right, I might end up just like them. "Apologies Raven. I wasn't sure my voice carried across the entire hall as I entered."

"You of all people need never apologize to me." Raven stood from the table. "What's on your mind?"

"The smell. Since the men of Cap Canna have been turned to…their more natural forms," Lexa said, trying to ease Raven's hatred of men, yet also trying not to fall from her favor. "Should we not put them outside the city? Pen them up in the hills? The stench of them will only get worse as the days pass."

"Right you are. I'll take care of it. Maybe we'll have a grand feast, we've yet to celebrate our new home."

"That's an idea, but I'm growing tired of eating them." In truth she'd not touched a single one, she'd been living off of Cap Canna's rich supply of fruits. Appearances mattered though, so she'd have to keep them up if there was ever to have a chance of convincing Raven, or possibly Sorsha, to turn the pigs back into men somehow. "But *I* like the pen idea. Cage them like the animals they already were. Let them live out their meager lives in despair of ever walking on two legs again."

"Aren't you the vindictive one? I like it." Raven turned to a woman at her side and said, "See that it's done, and send for Iliana."

"Yes, Raven." The woman bowed, then scurried out the room to carry out the orders.

"Now come, tell me what you know of Quazar." Lexa turned her attention back to the maps and pressed a finger on one.

"Quazar?" Lexa had to think hard to recall any tales of the city. "Not much, just rumors really. Nestled in the mountains across the bay to the east. Hardened people who seldom leave the land. Why? Planning on going there?"

"Many more sisters need liberation before I can carve out my kingdom."

Lexa frowned. "What's wrong with Cap Canna? I've never seen a place of such beauty before, and you've liberated plenty of sisters." Lexa found the words hard to say, but she forced herself to refer to the altered women as kin.

Raven laughed. "This island, as wondrous as it is, will not be part of it. No,"—Raven spoke to herself more than to Lexa as she continued running her finger over a map—"the world shall be my kingdom."

Lexa rounded the table, confused. She contemplated how Cap Canna could not be considered part of the world. Was it doomed like Atlantis was? Was it too destined to sink beneath the water? Raven knew more than she was letting on. Darla did too. Did these other women Raven had turned know something as well? They might not. Raven kept true to her word, as Sorsha would have, and did not pass on to them all the *gifts* she did to Darla. Not a woman in the city displayed anything close to Darla's crimson flash on the caravan route. But something from the gem had made it through to the other women. Lexa couldn't yet tell what, or if it was intentional on Raven's part to transfer some of the gem's sorcery onto them, but odd things had happened in the city. Things Lexa was certain would not have been tolerated in Cap Canna, especially after how the old woman upon first entering the city reacted to Raven's winged horsed. The Atlantean's, and their sorcery were feared by the people of every city Lexa had been too. And for good reason, not just because they were slavers, *the slavers.* But because of the sacrifices they would make of people, the torture they were rumored to inflict to further their arcane designs. Lexa had had her fill of sorcery even before she ventured to Cherteri, but more so since she'd experienced that sorcery first hand, and still is. But sorcery, none the less, was still upon her.

It was as if nature had become confused as to how to act. She'd seen dust swirls, small ones, appear and then vanish in the streets, torches flared for no reason, and the water in the bay had rippled the night before as if the land itself was in a constant state of shaking, but it wasn't. Raven passed something onto these women all right, something that didn't bode well for the world, Lexa feared.

Lexa brushed aside her thoughts and grounded herself, studying the map. "I can see why they seldom leave, and why any tales of Quazar is sparse. It's a perfect stronghold; the entire kingdom." Lexa paused at the word *kingdom* and glanced at Raven, hoping not to have sparked an irrational decision. She carried on before Raven could interrupt. "Mountains on three sides, a dense forest on the fourth leading to Oceans Lake." She ran her fingers over the lake, checked the legend on the map's edge. "If this map's accurate, it looks like it'd take a full day to cross Oceans Lake by boat just to reach the neighbouring…Cord…is it?"

"One expansion at a time my eager friend. The issue is, even with my prowess in battle, taking Quazar could make for a lengthy campaign. And the days run short if we are to liberate all our sisters. So, tell me, how would a thief take Quazar?" Raven lowered her brow, yet locked an intense gaze on Lexa.

A more perfect opportunity had not presented itself since Lexa had woke in the cave. "Solo," she said, in the utmost confidence "Two at the most." She blurted out her answer so fast that she hadn't yet processed what Raven had said about the days running short. It took a moment for her mind to catch up. The warm season had not yet peaked and the days were still getting longer. So, Raven's haste was not tied to the seasons. Lexa still had yet to pry what was so urgent from Raven since leaving the cave with Darla. Whatever the reasoning, it weighed on Raven.

"How could two take out an entire kingdom?" Raven frowned, pulling Lexa's attention back to the map.

"With ease." Lexa composed herself, let go of the whole haste issue, and proceeded with one of her favorite tactics: guile. "One of them is you. The other is me. With our skills combined they won't stand a chance. After all, this began with the two of us. It's fitting we should be the only ones to revel in the overthrowing of each kingdom, leaving each place we sack to the women who built it up. And if you convert them, *your* kingdom's survival will be fortified for all time. We can't lose." Lexa ran her finger over the map as if forming an intricate plan, yet secretly hoping Raven's ego had grown so much she would take the bait; leaving them alone long enough for her to tear the gem from Raven's chest as she slumbered. "Stealth will be key. I'll get you to the center of the city undetected, and you do what you've done to Cap Canna. I assume that *is* you goal."

"That's my girl." Raven wrapped her arm around Lexa's back, shaking her. "Wine!" Raven called out, her command echoing throughout the great hall. "This calls for a celebration. The original sisters are about to rid the world of its wickedness."

Lexa almost sighed relief at Raven's response. Sorsha would never have agreed to such a tactic, But Lexa had witnessed the brazen disregard of an opponent's skill by Xanatos. It appeared some of that disregard had an influence on Raven.

"You sent for me, Raven." Iliana entered the room.

"Indeed, come, join us."

Iliana waddled her way to the table, her perfectly trimmed shoulder length hair bouncing around her full cheeks. Even with Sorsha's prowess thrust onto her, Iliana still moved like a plump woman.

"Are you known in Zorin?" Raven asked.

"I am. Father thought it was necessary for me to gain the trust of our trade partners for when I take his seat at the throne."

Lexa restrained a huff, doubting there even was a throne. The city was run more by its people than by the king. From what Lexa heard, Iliana's father was basically in place so Cap Canna had a single voice. All in the city worked together, all had a say in what transpired within it, and with its trade partners.

"Tonight, you shall task a crew. Only two sisters. Tomorrow you set sail."

Lexa looked over the map, searching for Zorin, a city she knew nothing of. North of Quazar, past the copper cliffs, Zorin was isolated from the land on its own island.

"Dress in your bed robes"—Raven went on—"the same with the others. Take only the provisions you need to make the journey. You're to tell the people of Zorin that Cap Canna was attacked in the night by a grand caravan that *you* let into the city. One bearing wagons of gold and gems they claimed was for trade. The fortune was real, but the real reason they came was to take all you had to offer and add it to their pile of treasure. You narrowly escaped with your maids while the city was thrown into bondage."

Iliana bobbed her head up and down at Raven's every word. Lexa, though confused, waited to discover Raven's plan. Sorsha always had one, and her ways of obtaining that which she sought were cunning.

"Convince whoever you must to send a fleet of ships. Their biggest ones. The entire fleet if possible."

Lexa couldn't hold back any longer. "You want an entire fleet to come here? An army? Why?"

"Have faith, Sister," Raven said as polished gold cups filled with wine were brought to the map table by one of the sisters who left one before Raven, another before Lexa, and then began to distribute the remainder to the other sisters in the great hall.

Iliana, nor any other of Ravens "sisters" would question her tactics or her orders. But Lexa had to. If she was to save her friend and end this madness, she had to know everything Raven was setting up. Bringing a fleet of warriors to their door and being caught in a battle was the last thing Lexa wanted.

"You know I have faith." Lexa picked up a glass, swirled the wine in it, thinking. "But, why warn them? Why prepare *their* men to attack *us*?"

"Because they hunt whales."

"Whales?" Lexa asked.

"Yes, Sister. Whales. Zorin has the mightiest of ships, able to withstand the battering of the ocean far from land in pursuit of the animals. We need those ships. Those are the ones you're to bring to me."—Raven pointed at Iliana—"Do *not* return without the ships. Offer them all of Cap Canna's gold, the raider's gold, offer what you must. Do *not* fail me."

"Yes Raven." Iliana stopped bobbing her head and bowed low.

"Now go, prepare for tomorrow, and for a celebration tonight."

Iliana stood, and as fast as the woman could move without running, left the hall.

"If the tales of how big a whale is are true"—Lexa ran her finger along the map—"I doubt ships that large would fit down any riverways."

"They're as long as the ships you saw in Cherteri, the whales. And we don't need the ships for the rivers." Raven took a sip of wine, strode from the table and looked out the window to the bay. "They're to save us, and all the sisters we can free from the rough hands of men. Swine. As for us and Quazar. We should also bring Darla. She suffered at the loins of Thor, she's not from here, and she was my inspiration as to how I would grow my army. I want her with us."

Raven was done with talk of the ships, and Lexa knew it. "Agreed," Lexa said taking a gulp of wine. She'd soon have to kill the once timid Darla to save her friend. "There could be no better women for the job than the three of us."

Lexa hoisted her glass, and sat at the table studying the map. She wasn't concerned with their route to Quazar, that was simple and their plan was set, but what could Raven have in mind for the ships? Sailing inland was not an option due to their size, so they must be headed out to sea. West along the coast would take them back to Cherteri, east would take them to the place the ships made berth, Zorin. If that was Raven's destination why not just go there? Take Raven's force with her and attack them unprepared instead of warning them of a battle? No, Zorin wasn't Raven's target, Lexa decided. But what could it be then? Lexa's knowledge of this part of the world came from tales over jugs of wine with those claiming to have traveled here. In Lexa's trade as a thief she sought to learn as much as she could in order to choose her next target, and narrow down a place she would one day settle down at with a lifetime of riches. Cap Canna would have been a fine choice, but the more she thought of the ships, and the way Raven said the city wasn't part of the world, uneased Lexa's stomach, tightened it.

"Send for Darla." Raven commanded. A sister closest to the great hall's entrance nodded and left to carry out the order.

"And round up every horse in Cap Canna." Lexa added, her mind set more than ever that she has to succeed in putting an end to the Raven and her cryptic plans.

"Surely you don't want to head out this moment?" Raven left her place at the window and sat across the table from Lexa.

"Tonight, the warriors of the Raven shall soar in the sky to rejoice in our coming victory. They're key to what I've got in mind. Besides, ever since I saw your winged horse, I've wanted one of my own. That is if you can make more as magnificent as Xanatos did," Lexa said, provoking Raven's ego once again.

"They'll soar higher than ever." Raven's chin raised at the chance to show up the Last Atlantean. "An army of them."

"I can almost see it." Lexa feigned a grin, running through scenarios of the night to come, and the events that might present her a chance to free Sorsha from the Raven's grasp.

Chapter Eight

Thor stood at the bow of the ship with Lucius and Eric by his side. All of them staring as the city presented itself. The night sky had hidden the smoke of Tenzin from view, only to replace it with an eerie glow on the horizon.

"Tenzin isn't burning, it's burned." Lucius shook his head. "Why would Sorsha burn it to the ground?"

"Same reason she imprisoned all of Cherteri?" Thor tightened his grip on the rail. "Someone pissed her off."

"Not a hard thing to do," said Eric. "But if she's truly become impossible to deal with, I hope we have a plan other than charging at her with swords drawn."

"We do"—Thor put a hand on Lucius's shoulder, wobbling him back and forth—"here's all the plan we need."

"Me?" Lucius frowned.

Lucius' surprise reincarnation set tinder to Thor's fire of a plan. He'd used more than a few turns of the glass to mull over their next course of action as the ship meandered its way to Tenzin. He had vowed to save her, and Lexa, and in doing so possibly have Sorsha remove the curse placed on him, his traveling companions, and Cherteri if possible. But that would have involved him being able to tare that cursed Atlantean stone from Sorsha's chest himself; if that would even work. For him to do so he would have to convince Sorsha to let her guard down long enough so he could get within lunging distance of her. As smooth as he was in convincing people to come around to his views, such a task would prove difficult for even his skills due to his past with Sorsha. But having Lucius at his side is like having a hidden dice up his sleeve at the tavern tables.

"She fell for you, and the loss of you drove her to do this." Thor held out his palm toward what was left burning of Tenzin's buildings. "We put you before her, and she'll let down her guard. I'm sure of it. I'm also sure you're the only one she'll trust to get close enough to remove the gem from her chest."

"Your right, cousin. She'd never let either of us get that close. *Especially* you."

It was a jab at Thor as he could infuriate Sorsha like no other. He let it slide not only because it was true, but because he might be able to exploit that fact. "I could make for a good distraction, though."

"Or, you could fuel her rage." Eric nodded. "That's the last thing we need."

"It might be best to let her think you perished at the Red Ox," said Lucius. "Keep you out of sight, at least for initial introductions."

"I like that. But what of Lexa?" asked Eric. "She might be able to help us."

Thor hadn't considered her being of assistance. "She was able to calm you enough to ditch your fur once. Maybe she's already working her wiles on Sorsha, softening her up for Lucius. Though she doesn't know he's alive. One thing's for sure, we won't find her standing here." Thor crossed the deck to the steering wheel and turned the ship to come alongside the western river bank. As the ship moved into position so did he, letting go of the wheel and making his way to the bow of the ship he kicked loose the pin in the chain restraining the anchor from plunging into the river.

"He's never one to waste time, is he?" asked Lucius.

"There's no fun in it." Eric waited for the anchor to still the ship then slid a foot walk to the river's bank.

"Yeah, you two are related all right." Lucius loosed the mass of steel at his belt, snapping it with a flick of his arm into a bow, and stepped onto the foot walk.

Flames still licked the odd building, consuming what little remained that could catch fire. The city had been reduced to scores of skeletal stone frames, barren of all wood and nearly every clay roof. They made their way through the arch where gates of tall oak once stood. Smoke tickled the back of Thor's throat, caught in his chest. There would be no supplies to salvage, to barter for, nothing from Tenzin remained to add to the ship's hold. It was only good fortune that Lucius had outfitted it for their journey prior to their battle with Xanatos.

"It's like setting foot inside a spent camp-fire." Lucius kicked a glowing ember from his path.

Thor spit the ash floating in the air from his mouth into a pile of coals flickering in the night breeze. "This is a tomb," he said, looking down streets littered with sparks dancing across their cobbles. "Sorsha's long gone—didn't leave a soul alive."

"More accurately, to be found." Lucius walked backwards for a pace as he peered down alleyways. "There's no bodies. She was known for showing mercy even though she was the Raven."

Thor was impressed. Though Lucius had lost his soul, and the woman he loved had been torn from him to the point she barely resembled herself. The man still grasped hope with his tactical mind that Sorsha was unable of such destruction. Thor couldn't blame him, Lucius hadn't witnessed Sorsha's transformation, and he was always in search of a good time; always planning and looking for the positive outcome.

"I don't think Sorsha did this. The bite wound on my leg has been irritated since we hauled Eric on board. Come to think of it, since I ran into you at the Red Ox." Lucius frowned at Thor. "Must have been from the proximity to Cherteri and that cursed fog. But right now, I could scratch it until I reach the bone. Like the bite I suffered from Xanatos' wolf is telling me there's more touched by magic other than Eric here."

"Forget about your leg sniffing out sorcery." Thor scoffed. "We know this isn't natural. Blasted Atlantean did enough to us as it is." He clenched his fist, rubbing his fingertips over his palm where the scar from his blood-oath should be. All but Lexa had been afflicted by that cursed sorcerer. Denying it was useless, but that didn't stop Thor from being infuriated by it. He had lived by his wits, his strength, his speed, and his sword. Being touched by sorcery, more than a man, ate at him.

Lucius scratched his leg with his other foot and turned to Eric. "You said you could sense a wolf, control one. Can you feel anything now, sense those of your kind? Similar to how I can sense anything touched by Atlantean magic thanks to this infernal bite."

"It was more like I influenced it, not control it." Eric sighed. "It's worth a try." Eric held out his palm toward the city's center and closed his eyes.

"Well, anything?" Lucius asked, looking to the direction of the charred city Eric reached out to.

"Nothing." Replied Eric.

"Maybe you should stick to using your eyes, cousin." Thor drew his broadsword.

Rounding the corner three buildings away was a single gray wolf with silver-tipped fur. "The caravan." Thor cursed under his breath. Only Eric could have created these wolves. Left unchecked they in turn could create more like themselves surging a fur and fang filled plague across the land.

"I hate being right all the time." Lucius notched an arrow. The wolf crossed to the center of the street, locked its eyes on the trio of companions, and stood to its full height of six heads on its hind legs then spread wide its clawed fingers and bore its thumb length-fangs at them. "Why's it not attacking?"

Thor knew his target, where it was, what it was, but his gut and years of battle urged him to glance over rooftops, down alleyways, into building remnants. Anywhere an unseen threat might be hiding.

Eric stared at the wolf. "It's waiting. Waiting for—"

"Reinforcements." Thor raised his sword as a pair of wolves appeared down a side street. A dozen more popped out from between buildings. Some wolves bore their fangs, some snarled, and others stood. Thor tightened his grip on his broadsword. "Back to the ship. It's our only chance."

Lucius put an arrow in the first wolf's eye, sending the beast to topple back amongst its pack. "They've taken the entire city."

The wolves charged past their fallen brother.

"Move!" Thor shouted.

He pivoted his stance and began an all-out sprint for the ship. Eric overtook his pace, followed by Lucius, leaving Thor cursing and lagging behind. Fast as he was, he couldn't keep up to Lucius having being altered by Xanatos to be an "enhanced slave", nor to Eric with wolf blood running through his veins. They pulled away from Thor, meaning the wolves at his back were charging toward him faster than he could outrun them. Ten paces, twenty, then fifty paces separated Thor from the others. Infuriated, Thor pushed himself, pushed his speed to its limit. He pumped his arms as hard as he could, pushed his legs until they burned, all the while forcing his chest to maintain a steady rhythm of pulling in air. Many men had perished due to laboured breaths in battle, and that would not be the way he would falter this night. At such a pace a single loose stone could send him to the ground. He didn't dare a glance over his shoulder to know if he would make the ship before the wolves met him. The ship was his only chance.

Eric, a good seventy paces ahead of Thor, reached the river bank. He took the foot walk in two leaps, and Thor caught the order he barked. "Get to high ground with that bow," Eric cried to Lucius, pointing, and hauling up the anchor.

Fifty paces.

Lucius rushed to the steering wheel and spun it to pull the ship from shore, then he turned around, arrow notched, aiming over Thor's head. The arrow whizzed past Thor's ear.

A yelp sounded.

Lucius was deadly accurate. He always was, and from the distance of the wolf's death cry, Thor surmised that his friend's newfound strength had aided him in lengthening his range. Lucius loosed another arrow, the howl it produced was much closer to Thor's heels.

Thirty paces.

The ship pulled from shore.

Eric released the wheel, took hold of the foot walk, and held it tight to the rail.

Fifteen paces, almost there.

Another arrow flew past Thor's head, and his hair splattered with something warm and wet. He chanced a look behind him, finding a wolf collapsing just paces away with an arrow buried in its neck, and a pack of its brethren bounding past its corpse.

"Get on board!" Lucius shouted.

Thor didn't reply, he couldn't spare the air in his chest. He tightened his grip on his sword, and jumped for the retreating foot walk. He spun mid-leap, swinging his sword at the wolf leaping toward him, guiding the blade around a clawed hand reaching for him.

Steel bit into the wolf's flesh, then bone.

Thor landed with his back on the foot walk and the headless wolf on his legs.

Eric grunted from the impact on the foot walk. "Hurry up."

Thor kicked the wolf's decapitated carcass to the river, scurried up on all fours, and grabbed Eric's outstretched hand. The foot walk splashed into the water. Another wolf leapt from shore. Its clawed fingers and toes splintering the ship's hull, gouging deep scars in the wood, saving the beast from the water's current.

It slammed one clawed hand into the hull after the other, followed by each clawed foot, climbing for Thor's dangling feet.

An arrow in the shoulder dropped the wolf's arm to its side, yet it did not fall. The beast snarled, then locked its maw on the arrow's shaft, tugged it free and spit it into the river. It began to climb again, but Lucius' arrow slowed its advance enough for Eric to pull Thor on board.

"There's gotta be five score of them!" Lucius said, panic in his voice.

Thor scrambled away from Eric, back to the rail, held his sword poised to slash at the wolf's head as it climbed the hull.

Lucius buried another arrow in the wolf's chest.

The wolf's drooling jaw stopped snapping, and the light dulled in its eyes. Its hind legs sagged like dead weight, dragging its body down until the wolf clung to the hull with only one clawed hand. Its body slapped against the hull until it fell into the water with an unceremonious splash, leaving only the stain of its blood on the ship's side, and claw marks scratched against the grain of the wood.

On the bank, more wolves advanced from Tenzin, with no sign of their number dwindling. "The entire city's been turned." Thor said, forcing the image of a plague of wolves sweeping the world as far as the eye could see.

"I'm moving to the quarterdeck." Lucius dashed from Thor's side to the raised deck behind the main mast of the ship; an archers perch.

The first dozen wolves leading the chase reached the shore, churning up clumps of dirt behind them as they pivoted to keep pace with the ship catching the river's current and lurched forward. They didn't hesitate, springing for the ship, clinging to the hull as the first wolf had. Two failed to secure a hold, clambered against the hull then plunged into the fast-moving water of the Techa. A third flailed in the air, mid-jump, knocked off course from the arrow in its gut. "I'll never get used to how far they can jump," said Lucius, not pausing between shots from his elevated perch.

The wolves in the water struggled to keep their snapping maws above its surface. "They swim like babes though," Thor said to himself, then called out to Eric. "Drop the sail already. Get moving."

"Working on it." Eric was already tugging the lines loose that secured the sails as the first wolf made the rail.

Thor's broadsword sheared off the wolf's leg, dropping it to the deck, and its owner to the river.

Another wolf hauled itself up.

Thor sprang forward, driving his blade to the hilt in its chest, and shoving it back over the rail. His blade slid free from the thrashing wolf, and sliced through the air, hacking off a clawed hand, and lodging itself between furry ribs. Thor grunted in frustration as the pair toppled to the deck, the beast twitching its death throws and Thor reefing on his blade to free it.

"Goat loving son of a...the counterweights pinned in place!" Lucius shouted, then dropped a wolf to the deck with an arrow in its eye.

Though on his back, Thor understood what threat Lucius had discovered—the ship was listing. Lucius had designed the ship to haul great stones from the river without faltering, but Thor guessed the counterweights Lucius spoke of were an integral part of keeping the ship from capsizing.

Thor rolled the slain wolf from his chest, kicked his foot into it, and reefed his sword free.

Lucius abandoned his position at the rail of the quarterdeck, along with his bow, and made for an intricately designed table strung with a dozen ropes or more, each attached to a leaver and tied in place.

If Lucius was distraught, there was good reason for it.

Thor fought the urge to brace himself against the rail so he could maintain his footing.

Lucius was a good twenty paces away from him, and with wolves advancing the length of the hull Thor had two choices: Give Lucius the moments he needed to right the ship by defending him and letting Lucius work his mechanism by shifting the counterweights into position that would right the ship. That would mean abandoning the rail, pulling back to deal with the wolves closest to Lucius, and allowing the wolves climbing the hull before him to make the deck.

Or, beat Lucius to the end result of righting the ship, his way, by removing the excess weight brought on by the wolves. By putting his skills to the test, going blood-drunk, and slaying every wolf clinging to the hull.

The ship creaked and moaned as it tilted further, forcing him to adjust his footing as if he were in a battle on the downward slope of a hill; one where he had the high ground.

Thor chose the latter of his options.

He dropped his blade like a hammer between the eyes of a wolf cresting the rail. Its body fell, Thor braced his sword's guard against the rail, sliding it free of the twitching wolf. He planted foot on the rail and grasped it tight with his free hand, leaning over its edge he arced his broadsword at his nearest target. It carved a path from ear to opposite eye, relieving the beast of the top of its head and part of its snout. The wolf's furry shoulders shuddered as it went limp, and collided with one of its brother, sending the pair plumeting to be swallowed by the great Techa. Thor shuffled along the rail hacking at the next wolf below him, severing a hand from its owner. One made the rail a few paces from him, and that many paces closer to the unarmed Lucius. It flung itself on deck as Thor leapt, screaming, with his blade slicing down to split its skull. It sidestepped his blow and batted the honed steel aside. Thor landed at its feet, kept his momentum, and dove forward slamming his bracer and shoulder into a furry knee. The wolf yelped as its leg bent backward. Thor scrambled up the tilting deck, avoiding the wolf as it collapsed clutching its mangled knee with one hand and bracing itself on the rail with the other. Thor jumped, drove both his heels into the wolf's shoulder, and launched it over the rail as he fell to the deck. He pushed himself up, and peeked over the rail for his next target.

Beyond it, the remaining pack still on land plunged into the river having failed to leap the distance from the shore to the ship. Their fortunes were turning, no more wolves could make it aboard. The ship was beginning to right itself, be it from his efforts, or Lucius', or both, it didn't matter; he still had wolves clinging to the hull.

Yet another wolf launched over the rail with its clawed hand lashing out. He stood to skewer it on his blade but the beast pierced Thor's hardened leather breastplate. He fell back, pulling the claws free from his side and swinging his sword in desperation to put some distance between himself and the creature. Thor stabbed toward his aggressor. Before his steel could slick its blade further, another wolf crashed into his target and heaved it over the rail.

The wolf before him stood to its full height of seven heads, reaching a full head taller than the gray wolves clinging to the hull. Its size difference was immense, with much broader shoulders supported by layer upon layer of corded muscle, larger hands, and claws. Its fur was the same gray as the others, silver-tipped, but it also bore a long shaggy mane of deep crimson flowing along its back. The only oddity that the great wolf possessed—if there was such a thing aside from its existence—was a thin band of cotton about its waist, stretched to near its breaking point.

Eric had joined the fight.

Thor's heart both leapt and sank at the sight of his cousin coming to his aid—in wolf form.

Another gray wolf set foot on deck. It paid with its life as Eric removed its jaw and half its face with the single blow.

Thor scrambled to his feet, finding Lucius having set his counterweights and regained his bow, loosing an arrow from the quarterdeck. "We're losing ground," said Lucius.

Seven wolves counting Eric were on the deck. "Not if we can aim him." Thor indicated his cousin hunched between themselves and the advancing pack.

"His mind is altered the way he is. He won't recognize friend from foe. He's just as likely to turn on us as he is them without Lexa to sharpen his wits." Lucius fired another arrow over the rail.

The wolf closest to Eric lunged forward.

Eric caught it by the throat, stood to his full height hoisting the gray from the deck and drove his clawed fingers deep into its belly. The wolf thrashed wildly. Eric tore the wolf's ribcage from its body, spilling its guts and blood down his legs and over the deck. He tossed the limp carcass at two of its pack, sending the pair to the deck. Eric smashed the bangled ribs in the snarling face of another wolf as Lucius stuck it with an arrow in the throat, spilling its lifeblood.

"He's on our side," said Thor.

"Hope so, got five more still climbing. Lucius notched an arrow. "Last one."

At Lucius's words, Thor let out a battle cry and charged forward with his wolf cousin at his side.

He feigned right, drawing a slash of claws, then moved left with his own slash, severing a leg just below the knee. "One piece at a time." He couldn't help saying with hope, as that was exactly how they defeated Xanatos's giant winged wolf. His blade continued its path in an overhead swing, burying itself in between furry ears to a snout.

Eric took hold of his opponents' wrists, and tore both its arms free—one by the elbow, the other by the shoulder.

Eric kicked the armless wolf aside, and brandishing its limbs like clubs, became a torrent of fur and teeth. Blood spilled and bones broke as the wolf before Eric was reduced to a battered husk of limp flesh.

Another wolf leapt over its battered brethren, snapped its fangs, threatening to sink its teeth into Eric's shoulder.

Lucius's final arrow filled its gaping maw.

Eric looked over his shoulder at the arrowless Lucius, and tossed the arm torn at the elbow to Lucius's feet as if it were to be his new weapon.

"We know where you stand." Lucius nodded and drew his short sword. "I hope."

Eric dug his clawed feet and free hand into the mast and surged skyward, waving the arm he'd torn at the shoulder like a prize for the world to see.

He took hold of the rigging, and leapt.

"Get down!" Thor dropped to his belly, pulling Lucius with him. "He's not all wolf."

The rigging came taut, sending Eric swinging from stern to bow over the river, and the rope slicing through the air above Thor and Lucius's heads.

Using the dismembered wolf's limb like a club, Eric batted one wolf after another from the ship's hull. Reaching the bow, his weapon was no more than a drooping shell of meat filled with shattered bone.

The ship righted perfectly, no longer off-balanced by wolves.

Eric's chest heaved. The battle had been won, but he remained in a crouched attack position.

"This is a family matter," said Lucius, lowering his short sword, stepping back and away from Thor.

"Eric," said Thor, in as reassuring a tone as he could make. "Just breathe."

A deep growl sounded in Eric's chest, but didn't pass through his fangs, giving Thor hope he might be able to do as Lexa did, and calm the beast in control of Eric's mind.

Thor lowered his sword, straightened, and took a step sideways toward the rail. "Eric. Breathe." He took another step, sheathing his sword, and waved Eric over. "Come see. Come on."

"Eric's growl subsided, and he tilted his head to the side with what Thor thought could only be a confused wolf mind.

"Come watch the river…like we used to…as children…like you did coming down from the mountain." Thor rested both elbows on the rail and leaned over to gaze at the flowing water. His wager was a big one. Unarmed and exposing his back to a potential adversary with the ability to render him limb from limb was not a strategy Thor liked, but it was all he could think of to calm an alpha predator that once was his cousin.

Lucius didn't move a muscle.

Eric did.

He made his way across the deck on all fours still clutching his makeshift club, then he stood, mimicking Thor's posture.

Thor didn't break his gaze on the water below. Not even when wolves splashing along the shoreline drew Eric's attention. Thor cleared his throat, drawing Eric back to him. "Beautiful," Thor said, keeping his eyes lowered.

Eric looked from the wolves on shore to Thor, then followed his gaze to the water and its rhythmic movement and dropped the disfigured wolf's limb into the river.

Thor could have sworn half a glass had turned before Eric's crimson eyes rolled up into his lids and he collapsed to the deck with a dull thud. His fur thinned, shed, and blew away in the night breeze before it could catch in the sticky blood that soaked the wood beneath him.

Muscles shrank beneath thick hide that softened to become pink skin; bones snapped and reshaped themselves as Eric fell unconscious, yet still grunting at the painful transformation.

All that remained of the beast had slipped from sight. In its place Eric was naked, aside from the thin band of cotton about his waist, curled in a ball as a babe would. Sweat drenched him from head to toe, and as it poured from him, it washed away nearly every trace of his victims' blood.

For the first time in that half glass since he'd reached the railing, Thor loosened his grip on the dagger concealed beneath his bracer.

"Now what?" asked Lucius.

"We keep going till the Techa splits before the great ice flats it's fed from, and becomes the river Torin. Follow it to the city of Raich, and prepare an army for these beasts. For unless I miss my guess"—the wolves on shore kept pace, following the ship—"we've become their next target. If the great Techa and the Torin remain wide beyond the ice flats, they'll have to travel far to find a crossing to give chase. Just pray it's far enough to give us what we need to reach Raich."

Chapter Nine

"You want to explain to me how we're going to take Quazar if we're sailing in the wrong direction?" Raven asked, donned in her full battle armour, which was now transformed to match the purple attire she'd worn when she first became the Raven. "And for that matter, why are we even on this boat, I know we drank wine till the wee hours of the morning but didn't you say this would be an aerial assault?" She ran a brush over her winged horse's hair harder than needed.

"I did," replied Lexa from the bow. "Keep starboard if we're to miss those rocks."

"Star what?" Darla asked, craning her neck over the wheel.

"Veer that way." Lexa pointed. It was becoming evident Darla had no skills beyond that of a serving maid aside from the ones Raven had bestowed upon her. Which meant Raven may not have any sailing skills either. That could be something of an advantage. "I don't think I'll ever drink again. You're hard to keep up to when it comes to revelling, Raven."

"You knew that," replied Raven. "Now what of our route? I'm one for an adventure, but I'd still like to know the plan."

"We head south by ship toward Raich." Lexa picked up a brush to tend to her own winged horse.

"Raich? What about Quazar?" Raven frowned.

"The river forks North between here and Raich, empties into Oceans Lake, from there we take flight hugging the mountains to Quazar. We'll save our mounts for when they're needed. I know it seems like the long way around. Maybe it's the wine still in my system, but right now I like the thought of a prolonged journey. Besides, the view is endless with the rolling foothills and grasslands."

The longer the journey, the more chances she would have to free Sorsha. She tried to outpace Raven and Darla, get them to pass out from too much wine. Even pretending to drink while toasting the two women didn't accomplish that. Perhaps sorcery had a kind of dulling when it came to the effects of wine. Lexa had to shift her tactics, and wait for a chance to be alone with Raven. And on the journey, she might be able to pry free the reason for their haste. If not from Raven, then from the once-timid Darla.

~*~

It was early morning when the ship happened upon a village not large enough to be scribed on the maps—less than a score of thatch huts nestled in-between two foothills with a trail leading to the river and tiny fishing boats hauled on shore. Beside the two-man boats were three men sprawled out on the rocks. From their lack of reaction to Raven's ship approaching Lexa guessed the men were sleeping.

"Pathetic," said Raven. "No sense of grandeur. Just look at those oafs lying there on the rocks without a care in the world."

"No doubt pretending to work while their women slave away in those shanties." Darla nodded to the village. "About as useful as a pile of rocks, those men are."

With those words Lexa caught the corner of Raven's mouth turn up. As if she were concocting something unnatural for this unsuspecting village. "We should press on if we're going to make Ocean Lake by nightfall," Lexa said, attempting to take Raven's mind from the tiny village. Lexa pictured the shoreline with three pigs on it instead of three men.

"There's always time for a little fun. Stay with the boat if you like and keep it on course. I'll catch up." Raven climbed onto her winged horse.

"We'll catch up." Darla climbed onto hers.

Raven smiled. "Sure you don't want to join us? We could have this ship filled with more of our sisters in a turn of the glass. I know we said it'd be just the three of us, but why let any in my kingdom suffer when I can aid them?"

Lexa's hopes of freeing Sorsha diminished with Raven's words. A ship packed with warrior women, along with whatever animal the men of the village would be turned into made Lexa's stomach tighten. She had to flee, warn those ahead of her, prepare an army to counter the plague Raven would unleash on the land. "You go." Lexa stretched, hoping she looked unconcerned. Inside, her pulse raced. "I'll drop anchor and wait for your return. If we're to celebrate your liberation of this village I'm sure you'll want to delight in some revels tonight, and I'm not ready for another night trying to keep up to you without a rest."

"Rest up then. Be ready to welcome our sisters." Raven kicked her mount and took to the air.

"Just be back by sundown."

"Done," replied Raven. "Come on Darla."

Lexa watched as the pair flew to the shore and dismounted, startling the three men lounging on the rocks to the point Lexa was sure one of them soiled himself from his reaction. What followed, Lexa would never have guessed.

Raven had taken Darla's words to heart. Caressing the nearest man's chin with her hand, Raven bore him to the ground with but a touch. Leaving him crying out in agony, a cry that grew deep and hoarse as his flesh turned to stone.

"Oh Sorsha," said Lexa as Raven moved for the next man. What Lexa thought were to be statues of men became much more. They grew to twice their normal height and just as wide. With broad shoulders and sloping foreheads above tiny lifeless eyes. The men stood where they were changed, like guardians of the village. Either unwilling or unable to move, they remained expressionless as the third man ran for the village, screaming with Raven and Darla strolling after him without a care in the world.

"I need help," said Lexa, taking hold of the wheel and continued south toward Raich, leaving them behind.

Chapter Ten

Eric opened his eyes to a sun hanging high in the sky. The gentle rocking back and forth along with the smell of fresh water told him he was still on the ship. "I'm guessing we made it out of Tenzin?"

"Thanks to you, old friend," said Lucius from the wheel. "But don't do that again. We've got enough to worry about without adding you eating us to the list."

"Looks like you figured out how to turn all toothy, now if you could just figure out how to control yourself. Well, let's just say that'd be helpful," said Thor between bites of a dried strip of meat.

"You all right?" Eric asked Thor at the sight of his blood-stained sleeveless shirt on the deck beside his form fitted breastplate, which now bore four long gashes in it.

"Oh, he's better than alright. Seems Xanatos's creature is the gift that keeps on giving. Wish Xanatos was as generous to me," said Lucius, his last words less upbeat than his first.

"What do you mean?" Eric stood, confused, partially from Lucius's words, and partially from the fog still lingering in his mind from the night before.

"Well…I got cursed without a soul and a leg that gets pissed off around your type," Lucius replied. "You got to become basically immortal with how you can heal…aside from the whole turning to a wolf thing that's not too bad. But him." Lucius nodded at "He got the best of it all."

"Best of what?"

To which Lucius replied by pulling out his dagger. "This." He tossed it at Thor's back, burying the blade below Thor's right shoulder."

"Lucius!"

"Ahh!" cried Thor. "I'll addle your wits!" Thor fell to the deck, and hammered his fist on it, coughing.

Eric pulled the dagger free, balled up Thor's shirt, and pressed it against the wound.

"No need for that," said Lucius in an almost jealous tone.

Thor raised his palm toward Eric indicating him to stop. He spit a wad of dried meat mixed with blood onto the deck. "Really, Lucius? That's too far."

Thor rose to his feet, fists clenched. Eric had seen that look before on his cousin. One that meant Thor was about to teach someone a lesson, not with a blade, but with his bare hands.

"What? *You're fine.*" Lucius dismissed Thor with the wave of a hand. "Better to show him than tell him anyway."

Eric looked at Lucius, then to Thor's wound. The blade Lucius had thrown left no trace of ever being stuck in Thor's back. Eric wiped the trickle of blood running from where the wound had been, ran his fingers over the spot that should be a hole in his cousin's back, not even a scar presented itself. "Closed shut, just like the ones on the wolves did; just like *mine* did."

Thor shrugged Eric's hand off.

"That's right. You two are gonna live forever, provided you can keep your heads."

"Do that again and I'll break you in half." Thor grunted, restraining himself. "He's pissed how he and Sorsha ended up. In truth I can't blame him," Thor said to Eric, then scowled at Lucius. "But that's enough." Thor rolled his shoulder, stretching where the blade had pierced him.

Eric looked at Lucius using the wheel to support himself. He's been into the wine. A lot of it. But that doesn't explain what he did, and why Thor's not beat him to a blubbering mess by now.

"How's this possible?" Eric asked. "And what's with him? I've not known you to show restraint, especially for what he just did."

"Best we can figure is like Lucius said, Xanatos' winged wolf. Before we killed it, Kane's blade went through it and sliced my ribs. Didn't think much of it at the time, was so close to where it clawed me, I just bandaged my side up before taking the women back to Cherteri."

"You never noticed you could heal so fast?"

"After Sorsha leveled the Red Ox, I ached all over, but with no blood running down my side I didn't check the wound until I found the ship."

"And my wine. You're welcome for that by the way." Chimed Lucius as he took a swill of wine from a jug.

Thor shot him a look and continued on. "I made a blood-oath at the Ox." Thor squeezed his fist. "It healed, but it wasn't until that wolf opened me up last night that Lucius here realized I had no scar from Kane's blade, nor from the wolf. As for him,"—Thor nodded at Lucius, and spoke in a hushed voice to Eric—"he's been like a bitter old man all morning, and hitting the wine hard. I've been waiting for you to rise. Get your take on him."

"I've half a mind to let *you* bite me"—Lucius sneered at Eric, cutting Thor off—"might let me last long enough to figure out how to get my soul out of this thing." Lucius slurred as he hefted up a crimson stone and peered at it before the sun.

Glimmering as if a thousand tiny suns were trapped beneath its polished surface, Eric recognized it as a piece of Xanatos' sorcerous gem.

"What are you doing with *that*?" asked Thor, stepping forward.

"Better in my hands than in someone else's who can do sorcery and such." Lucius examined the gem shard closer. "'Sides, part of *me* is in there. And I found it first."

"Lucius." Eric stepped forward. "You heard what that thing did to Sorsha. Xanatos is still part of it, dead or not. It's too risky to keep around."

"No, cousin. Lucius is right, we can't let that fall into the wrong hands."

Thor's words made no sense to Eric. Xanatos's gem, even a piece of it, was far too dangerous.

"Finally, something intelligent comes from the barbarian's mouth," said Lucius.

Soft enough for only Eric's ears, Thor whispered, "Or *any* hands for that matter. Its touch could be addling his wits more than I want to do to him myself. Like the other shard did to Sorsha." Thor nodded to Lucius. "He's only become belligerent since he figured how I heal. Musta been thumbing it all morning."

"Might be right," said Eric just as quiet. "I've drunk with him plenty to know he's not usually like this. No matter how he felt or how much he drank, he'd never have put a knife in you."

"What are you two going on about? Whispers are lies you know. Or are you plotting to take my gem from me?" Lucius held the plumb-sized stone to his chest.

"Take the gem. Knock him out if we have to," Eric whispered.

"Doesn't heal like us." Replied Thor.

"Gently then."

"Go."

The cousins crossed the deck to Lucius so fast the only thing he could get out was, "No, it's mine, you can't—" before Eric grabbed him by the wrists, sending Lucius's jug to shatter on the deck.

Thor swung the pommel of his dagger across the back of Lucius's head. Lucius's eyes rolled back and Eric caught him before he fell on the clay shards from the jug.

"What happened to gently?" Eric asked.

"He didn't stick a dagger in your back." Thor eyed the crimson gem on the deck, squinting deep in thought as if weighing his options as to what to do with it. He dumped out his coin purse and scooped up the gem, being sure not to touch it. Tying the top, he held up the purse shaking its contents before his cousin. "He doesn't get this back until he's of the right mind, and it stays in the purse."

Eric searched Thor's eyes for a hint of madness. None came. Nor did any words not fitting of his cousin like what had happened to Lucius. Thor's gamble about not touching the gem was right, Eric decided.

"Agreed."

In truth, he was relieved he didn't have to fight his cousin. Eric had never bested Thor in all their years growing up together, and even with the wolf in him he wasn't sure he could.

"What about him?" Thor tucked his purse beneath his belt.

"Let him sleep it off, if he wakes still charged up, I'll take care of it."

"Good. Cause I'll have my hands full convincing the people of Raich that there's a war coming to them."

Eric turned around; they'd reached the city of Raich.

Chapter Eleven

Lexa waited, patiently, in King Cinna's chambers. Hooded with a cape on her back, she was dressed for stealth and silence. Leaning against the bed rail in the shadows, her face was veiled so her white skin and red lips were cloaked in darkness; only her icy-blue eyes would give her position away. She'd donned her full battle armour comprised of soft leather shoulder pads, breast plate, bracers, and greaves all dyed black, and she stood as poised as any seasoned warrior emanating confidence.

The king of Raich opened the door to his bed chamber, his bulging belly entering the room first. He made it three paces before ceasing whatever errand he was running, and Lexa took a step forward. King Cinna jerked, froze in place, and eyed her from head to toe. "Well, isn't this nice?" The king of Raich straightened his white robe spackled with fine lace sewn to resemble waves, and dropped his hand to his side; just beside his dagger. "Whose purse did you fill with gold so that you may gain my favor?"

The king strode to a mirror on the wall, keeping a steady eye on Lexa. She waited, sizing him up. If he was a warrior once, he'd grown relaxed, fat, and from his gait Lexa surmised he'd grown slow as well. She remained silent, wanting to see the king's reaction to her, letting him have a semblance of control in his own bed chamber. Let him relax.

Cinna stared at her through the mirror and stroked his beard with one hand. The other hand never more than a few finger breadths from the dagger on his black gilded belt. He turned to face her. "Have you come to put me to bed, I think not dressed like that. I'd wager you're here to rob me. So, if I were you, I'd think carefully on your next words as they may be your last."

Lexa took another step forward, and the king took one step back. Intimidating the big bellied king was almost too easy for her to enjoy it. "You're right, oh wise king. The name's Lexa, and I am a thief. One good enough to slip past your guards undetected. But I'm not here to take from you, I'm here to give you something; information. I sought an audience with you, and your personal guards wanted nothing to do with what I had to say. You'll find them slumbering in the garden to wake with sore heads."

King Cinna frowned.

"See for yourself." Lexa held her palm out to the doorway behind her.

King Cinna hesitated before wresting his hand on his dagger and walking past Lexa to the balcony overlooking the garden. "They're my finest men, and you bested them alone?" He ran his fingers through his graying black hair, then down to stroke his beard again.

"They *were* your finest." Lexa corrected him. "And yes, I bested all four of them. Now you know who is in your chambers, and that I'm not here to steal from you, or to kill you. If I was, you and your men would not rise again if I deemed it necessary."

Lexa waited for her words to register with the king as she lifted her short sword from its soft leather scabbard, revealing its blued steel. Knowing that if King Cinna had any knowledge of thievery, her garb ensured she could slay him and slip out of the castle without being detected, be it day or night, not even her blade would reflect light to give away her position.

"Will you hear me out?" Lexa dropped her blade back in its scabbard.

"I suppose I don't have a choice. Lexa…was it?"

"Good, now pour us some wine." Lexa pulled her veil down, flipped her hood back, and sat on a chair layered in fluffy cushions.

King Cinna raised an eyebrow—an expression she was used to when men set eyes on her—then he picked up two cups and a gold jug from a table against the wall. "I'm not used to being spoken to like *that*. But something tells me you're used to speaking to Royalty in such a manner."

"Let's just say yours is not the first chambers I've entered that has had the title as royal, earned or not." Lexa took a sip of the wine King Cinna handed her, then placed the cup on an end table beside her. "Let me start in the beginning, in the city of Cherteri."

King Cinna drank three cups as Lexa laid out the battle against Xanatos, the fall of Cherteri, and the threat of Raven soon to come. When she was finished, she picked up her own cup, drained it, and asked, "So, what say you?"

"Um." King Cinna said, with a clear expression on his face of disbelief. "I think you're mad." He jumped up from his chair and dashed for the doors. "Guards!" he called out.

Lexa pursed her lips, breathed out a heavy sigh, shaking her head. "You're gonna pay for that." She stood and made for the balcony doorway, not rushing. Before stepping through, she warned him once more. "But not by my hand. Raven's coming whether you believe it or not, and I was your only hope for survival. Goodbye foolish King."

Guards rushed into the King's chambers. Lexa hopped over the balcony, slid down the rope she'd used to gain access to King Cinna's chambers, landed, rolled, and sprinted through the royal garden filled with berry bushes and apple trees. She hauled herself over the shoulder-height castle wall with shouts from the guards sounding the alarm.

Traversing alleys and streets she reached the wharf lined with fish markets, inns, and taverns. She altered her pace to match that of the citizens of Raich mulling about. With her ship in sight, and checking she'd evaded any guards giving pursuit—of which she'd seen none—she cursed the king, silently. Why some men, especially kings in her experience, had heads harder than the walls they lounged behind she'd never know. Perhaps Sorsha was right. Most men were oafs, whiling away their lives in search of gold and a bedding. They didn't deserve what Raven had in mind for them, but Sorsha wasn't entirely wrong in her take of them. Some *were* different though, not many, but some.

Eric, and how he jested, lived free as she did, and enjoyed her company aside from being pressed together in the throes of passion was one of those men. The thought of him, and how he differed from most, warmed her chest. He was hers, and she was his. They shared an unspoken natural bond—one born out of a chance encounter plying their identical trades—one that strengthened as days passed.

She chuckled about how they met trying to raid King Isak's coffers, and about how she thought him less than an adequate thief, at first. He'd proved her initial take on him false, and also proved himself worthy to be by her side. Her chest tightened. She'd never see him again, never feel the warmth of his body pressed against hers. She knew what she needed, what she yearned for, and sought out that which would slake her anger, her grief. A roughly carved sign depicting a bear dancing with overflowing cups in its paws presented itself, and she turned toward the tavern.

~*~

"While you're waiting for him to come to." Thor nodded at the unconscious Lucius sprawled out on the deck. "It might be wise to spread out the gold around the ship in the chance we have to leave it unattended."

"Just get going." Eric waved off his request as only his cousin could do.

The scent of freshly caught fish on display brought back memories of the last time Thor set foot on the docks of Raich. It'd grown since his last visit. Half a score of docks lined the natural cove carved by the river Torin. Taverns and inns had spread further along the boardwalk to mix their distinct aroma with the fish markets; now running two streets deep lined with cobblestone roads before reaching Raich's city walls.

Standing twice the height of a man they were formidable walls, yet nothing compared to Cherteri's grand defenses. Archers spread along the top would be useful if their numbers were increased for when the wolves arrived, Thor thought, inspecting the defenses sightlines popping in and out of view between buildings in the distance.

Making his way through the city of merchants and artisans brought a smile to his face, especially when passing the taverns he'd frequented. Taverns he'd spent many a night in dicing and befriending the comely maids that performed on stage re-enacting legends of the past. He wondered, if some day, if the city survived, if they would sing songs and act out the adventures *he'd* been through.

Thor approached the guards leaning up against the castle wall. "I seek an audience with the king." Like the archers, and his nature, Thor assessed what lay before him. The castle walls, only standing shoulder height, were more for show as the small castle behind it was barely worth protecting. Standing no taller than an inn with a single set of stairs, the castle's walls were more of a status symbol than anything.

"He's busy." One of the gate guards replied.

"As will you be tonight." Thor tossed a purse of gold coins at the guard. "All I require is my announcement."

The guard hefted the purse, looked inside, and his eyes grew. It was obviously more than he'd expected for a simple introduction.

"What do they call you?" The guard tucked the purse from sight, stood, and turned toward the castle.

"Thor."

He followed the guard through a garden barely large enough to accompany a team of horses before coming to stone stables. Inside the castle, Thor was led up the staircase, and after the guard rapped on wooden doors, he was announced to the king. "My Lord, may I present Thor of…" He paused, and looked at Thor.

"Of Falun." Thor stepped through the door held open by the guard.

"Of Falun." The guard repeated.

The King looked at the guard, then to the purse bulging at his belt. "What business do you have with me, Thor of Falun?"

"I bring news from Cherteri, and a warning."

"Let me guess, a crazed woman wielding the power of Atlantis." I have to hand it to you, sticking to your story. I'll not be robbed by the likes of a Barbarian and his harlot. You should have timed your visitations better. Arrest him."

The guard Thor had bribed, along with a pair inside the king's chambers, drew their swords.

Thor kept his gaze locked on the king, not moving a muscle. "Try it…and they'll be on the flat of their backs before you can take a step. That oath I'll swear here and now."

"Guards."

The one Thor had bribed stepped forward and was rewarded with Thor's boot kicking the wind from his gut, slamming him against the wall. A guard to the left swung his sword at Thor's neck. A slash Thor leaned back from to let the blade slice only air. Thor lunged forward, punched the guard in the throat, sending him to the floor gasping. Thor continued past the fallen guard, out of reach of the last one still standing. He drew his broadsword, letting the heavy blade whoosh through the air. The sign of such a heavy piece of steel being wielded so effortlessly had the same effect on the guard as it had on so many before—fear.

The guard swung his sword out of desperation to end the fight fast. A move Thor expected, and batted aside with ease, then he hammered his pommel into the guard's nose. The man dropped to his knees, hands covering his face, with blood pooling in his palms and spewing to the floor.

Thor kicked a chair across the room, snapping an ornately carved leg off as it crashed against the wall. "Now," he said in a calm voice, and pointed the tip of his broadsword at the king. "You're going to tell me before I choose to swear another oath. What harlot do you speak of that's warned you?"

"I…ah." The king croaked through a throat that'd lost all moisture.

"What's it going to be?" Thor pointed his broadsword at the floor and stood tall—a good handsbreadth above the king—using not only his size to further intimidate the man before him, but displaying a confidence that he could drop his guard and still prevail as well.

A fourth guard ran into the doorway. The king cleared his throat. "Stand down."

"My Lord?" the guard questioned.

"See that they're tended to." The king nodded to the men on the floor. "We've business to discuss he and I."

The three men were collected and helped down the stairs, leaving the king and Thor alone.

Thor tossed another purse of gold, letting its coins spill along a table. "For the chair." Thor was never one to be cordial, but he knew it would ease the king's unrest. Threats, displays of strength, of prowess, all bent men to compromise, to listen, but gold coerced them into doing it willingly.

The king looked at the broken furniture, then the gold, then to Thor. His eyes losing their grip on fear, gaining their grip on greed. "Thor of Falun…was it?"

Thor bowed, sheathing his sword.

"Cinna. I think you and I are past formalities."

"Agreed." Thor walked over to a table and hefted a gold jug. "Now what about this harlot you speak of?"

"Cinnaaa!" shouted a voice from beyond the balcony leading to the garden, a female voice filled with rage.

Thor stepped onto the balcony.

"Cinnaaaaaaa!" shouted the voice again.

Silhouetted by the sun was a lean long-haired figure hovering above the garden on a winged horse. "Sorsha." Thor drew his sword, bent his knees, prepared to leap clear of whatever unnatural thing she was sure to send his way.

"Thor?" the voice said, softening, yet trading anger for excitement. "Thor!"

With the voice void of anger, Thor recognized it immediately and shielded the sun from his eyes with his hand. "Lexa."

Chapter Twelve

Raven's winged horse touched down in the shore of Cap Canna's Bay. She jumped off her mount, the water cooling her legs, and her temper. Standing she found three of her sisters rushing to greet her, each with looks of confusion on their faces.

"Back so soon?"

"Where's Lady Lexa?"

"And what of Darla?"

"You couldn't have reached Quazar to make it back by now."

Raven raised her hand, silencing the barrage of questions, not one of them asked without overlapping another from a different sister. "Lexa's betrayed us, Sisters."

"What?"

"No."

"Your second?"

"She fled before we could make the journey. Darla is to take care of my…friend, the traitor," Raven said, prompting nods from the three women. "Do not fret, I have my trusted subjects, my sisters. No other can be trusted," she said more to herself than the women parting way for her to step on shore.

"We have news that might brighten your spirits, Raven," the youngest of the three said.

"Impetuous youth. You should be flogged for claiming to know what I want." Raven paused, considered the girl, decided she would give her one more chance to prove her wits and forgo her stupidity. "What?"

"When we took Cap Canna."

"*We?*" Raven leaned closer to the girl.

"Beg your pardon, Raven." The girl corrected herself, bowing her head. "When you freed us from our bondage of Cap Canna."

"That's more like it." Raven held her pose, waited a moment for the girl to gaze at the ground, then Raven stood straight. "Continue."

"Three ships escaped the bay's opening to the ocean." The girl pointed north to the wide expanse of water surrounded by the bay's cliffs.

"How's that supposed to make me happy?"

"They must have reached Zorin, and spread word of what happened here. We sent ships out, trailing Iliana so they could return with word of her dealings there. It seems the tales of Zorin's hatred for sorcery was true. Your power has enraged them. They were isolated, far from Atlantis…and…you being so close to them—"

"Spit it out girl before I put you down myself." Raven curled her fingers around the smooth leather of her sword's handle.

The girl's eyes darted from Raven's face to the sword, then back again. "A fleet of ships is approaching as we speak. Each heavily armed. I thought it would lift your spirits to dispatch the stinking sailors coming to set foot on your kingdom. They should be within sight by mid-day." The girl dropped her gaze, remained silent.

"I should never have doubted you," Raven said, waiting for the youth to raise her head again. "Next time, get to the point."

"Yes, Raven. There is one other thing."

"*What* did I just say?"

"Iliana's ship never made the journey. It was met by the fleet in open waters."

"Killed or captured?" Raven shut her eyes, breathed heavily to alleviate the heat flushing her.

"Those that trailed her couldn't tell. Iliana's ship was attacked, boarded, and sunk. If our sisters were taken back to the fleet, we don't know."

Raven looked over the three women standing poised, waiting for her command. "Come, we have work to do." She turned toward Cap Canna and started walking. The three women followed, keeping pace, waiting for instructions. "We've uniforms to prepare. No army of the Raven's should be donned in everyday clothing. Gather our sisters to the docks. Be sure they're well-armed with both blade and bow. We'll rescue Iliana if she lives."

"Yes, Raven."

"Right away, Raven."

"By your command, Raven."

The women took off running, shouting in different directions, giving Raven a moment to herself. Her plan was coming to fruition, as she knew it would. But the one thing, the only thing she didn't expect still gnawed at her. Lexa. She couldn't help but think of how she and Lexa had fought so well together, of how she had named the thief her second, of how they were like kin, of her desertion, of her betrayal. "Oh Lexa, how I wanted you here at my side? Guess I'll have to settle for just your head when Darla returns."

~*~

The Raven's force had dispersed between the docks and the boats bobbing in the bay, all her sisters waiting for her command. Standing atop an elevated platform on shore, she surveyed the army she'd split into three waves.

The first stood, armed with sword and bow, on Cap Canna's dozen or more boats. Though not war ships like their opponents, they looked formidable thanks to the warriors aboard, and how could they not be, having been blessed with her skills, thought Raven. Surrounded by fishing nets littering the decks of boats that'd never left the bay's abundant waters hardened women waited for battle, confident of the victory to come.

The second wave sat on winged horses on the dock's ends. Each woman wielding a bow and a full quiver on their backs.

The Third and final wave stood on the rocky shore beneath her perch.

"Today, sisters," Raven said, pointing to the fleet of war ships entering the bay. "Today we cleanse these waters of the swine that dare to enter them."

Shouts of agreeance filled the air.

"Today you shall make me proud, proving your worth to not only me, but to yourselves as well, and you shall do so bearing my crest." Raven raised her palms toward the ships. The shard in her chest flared crimson, surging power to her palms and shot out, bathing the army below her. "And you shall look the part of true warriors as well." The power and the crimson hue, faded, drew back into the shard. The crimson hue encircling her warriors altered their garb as it faded away.

Robes, tunics, and dresses alike, all transformed appearance and material before her prideful gaze.

Crimson cloaks flapped in the wind. Triple plated armour made of brushed steel covered every shoulder. Widespread wings of a raven covered matching breastplates. Interlocking armour concealed torsos. Wide leather straps hung halfway down thighs, and polished bracers and greaves gleamed in the sunlight.

Renewed shouts and cheers echoed off the bay's walls.

"That's better," Raven said to herself, satisfied her sisters bore armour that matched hers. "Weigh anchor, scuttle the small ships, and commandeer the larger sea-faring vessels. And remember, Sisters, one ship at a time." Raven swiped her hand out before her and created a blast of air.

Oars plunged into the water. Sails unfurled, caught the wind she sent forth. Outnumbered two to one, her warriors held their composure with every tug of the oars. The enemy's flagship, manned by at least fifty men Raven gauged, towered over the largest her fleet had to offer, falling short of a score of women packed between the rails.

"Off goes the bait." Raven said to herself, waiting, watching the gap shrink between forces.

"To the air!" she commanded, pointing to her sisters waiting on their winged horses.

Wings beat. Mounted horses rose into the sky.

"Let no man survive," Raven murmured.

Battle cries sounded. Screams of enraged sisters, fuelled with a blood-lust Raven knew only too well, echoed off the bay's high cliff walls. Zorin's flagship, so brazen to be the first to enter her waters, would be the first to fall.

Spears soared from their flagship to her boats surrounding it, then were sent back to where they came from, hurled by her sisters. Men swung down on ropes, steel flashed, flickering sunlight back from the decks. Arrows rained down from her winged force dispatching targets on both her ship and her enemies. A net soared through the air, its hooked end caught the deck and rail of Zorin's flagship forming a ladder. Her sisters climbed.

Composed, poised with hand on hilt, ever diligent, Raven looked on, waiting to give her next command. The fishing net used as a makeshift ladder, the ingenuity of it, tugged at her. The idea was hers, but it was a feat worthy of...Lucius.

Lucius...his soft smile...his eyes...his touch, came back to her, flooded her. All their moments together blurred, became one, and assaulted her senses; overwhelming her. Raven shuddered, struggling to release a choppy breath along with her beloved's memory surfacing from within. Lucius once had held her heart, and even though he'd perished, he still had a grip on her. A tug-of-war game went on in her mind. One pulling her from the scene of carnage unfolding before her, and drawing her to the very soul of her beloved. She traced her fingers along the shard embedded in her chest, and a warmth overtook her. A wave that flushed her cheeks as if she were back in his embrace.

"Raven. Raven." A voice repeated, but it wasn't his, wasn't Lucius's. No, he didn't call her Raven, he never had. Her name was...she couldn't remember.

"Raven!" Shouted a woman, shaking her by the shoulders, snapping her back to the reality of this world.

"*What?*" Raven barked, enraged from being pulled from such a moment of bliss.

"Our sisters are being overrun." The woman released Raven's shoulders, stepped aside.

"No," said Raven.

How long had she drifted? How long had she forsaken her sisters for a memory like that of a fleeting dream?

Her fleet...was surrounded.

The flagship remained manned. Three of her boats were empty or littered with her fallen sisters. "No," Raven repeated, looking to the sky. She was no archer, therefore nor were her sisters bearing bows. There were too many to count that had fallen, leaving the rider-less winged horses scattering in the wind.

"No!" she screamed, leaping down from her perch to the pebble beach, and stomped her foot on the water, turning its surface to ice beneath her boot.

The ice, though only three handsbreadths wide, shot from beneath her foot toward the fleet so fast it made its own wake as it went. Faster than a ship could sail, faster than her horses could fly, the strip of ice surged forward, carving a path through the water, and encased Zorin's flagship's hull. Raven threw her hands up in the air, and the flagship followed suit, hoisted from the water's surface on a column of ice, scattering her remaining winged fleet.

"Into the water," Raven commanded, fists clenched, nails digging into palms.

"My lady?" questioned the woman who had shaken her.

"Now!"

The women on shore raced forward, splashing into the water up to their waists on either side of Raven's make-shift ice trail. Raven hammered her fists on the ice, and the entire length of it from her fists to the ship blazed crimson. The thin ice-path melted away, tainting the water with trails of crimson power snaking toward every sister partially submerged before her. Rage filled her heart, and she imbued the waters she'd created with that rage. One by one, as each sister was surrounded by crimson at their hips. Raven sensed that same rage burning beneath her chest within each of them, and she grinned as the water below them flashed. The flash vanished, the crimson tainted water faded, diluted by the bay, and left forever changed bodies in its wake.

"Go forth, Sisters of the sea," Raven murmured, stumbling back, drained of energy.

Her sisters dove into the water. Scales on what were once legs glided beneath the surface, followed by fins that used to be feet. They swam as fast as any creature of the sea, swarming the nearest ship, and capsizing it.

Cries for aid filled the bay. Cries of men with fear in their hearts.

"Use your gifts," Raven said, softly, but not to herself. "*My* gifts." Her words floated in the air, whispering in the ear of every member of her army.

The wind gusted, concentrated in blasts sent forth from her sisters still alive on the boats, knocking men from their ships. Balls of fire formed in the palms of what remained of her winged warriors and rained down on their enemy. Plumes of water rose, carrying her sisters of the sea, up and over ships, pulling men down to the depths.

"You're safe," Raven said, dropping to her knees, disgusted with herself for falling victim to a man's distraction, even…*his*. "Never again."

Chapter Thirteen

Lexa's winged horse landed with a thud in the garden. No sooner had she dismounted than she was in Thor's embrace on the balcony having scaled a rope she tossed to its rail on her decent.

"It's good to see you too," Thor said as he waited for her to break their embrace.

"Sorsha told me you were dead." Lexa pulled back, looking him over.

"Not for a lack of trying." Thor smirked. "And I'm not alone, Eric's with me as well."

"*Truly?*"

Thor nodded.

His simple gesture hit her hard. Her eyes watered. She turned from Thor to look out over the city. A proud woman, Thor thought, with knowledge of Eric being alive she still held her composure. At least to the point of not letting anyone see her lose it. "My cousin's a lucky man, far too undeserving of a woman such as yourself." Thor leaned on the rail beside her enough to catch the grin he prompted from her. "I'll take you to him soon enough. First we have to prep Cinna here or else our reunion will be short-lived."

"He knows all I do. Didn't want to listen much, though." Lexa glared over her shoulder at the king. "I planned to drop in with my winged horse to prove I wasn't mad like he claimed."

"I apologize, Lexa, your tale about Cherteri and Atlantis seemed that of a child's imagination. I was sure of it. But your mount, and now with Thor's brutish entrance. You have my undivided attention as to how we're to stop this…Raven…was it?" King Cinna asked.

Ignoring the king, Lexa looked over the room, her eyes stopping briefly at the broken furniture and the blood pooled on the floor. "Didn't think I'd find you here, Thor. I see you had no trouble seeking an audience either."

Thor grinned, she was an observant woman, this one, and a warrior at heart. His cousin was indeed a fortunate man to have found such a woman, and one that was willing to put up with him, let alone his condition. "You have your ways and I have mine."

"And we're going to need both of them if we're to stop Sorsha."

"I'm almost afraid to ask." Thor jumped up to sit on the railing. "Where have you been, and what's she been up to?"

"She took Cap Canna, and I mean took it. A piece of Xanatos's stone is lodged in her chest. Gives her power like his. She gave Cap Canna's women battle skills to match hers, warped their minds to hate men."

"Great."

"That's not the half of it. She turned all the men into pigs. Others she turned into giants like those you fought at Cherteri's bridge, only these are made of stone." Thor shook his head at her words. Sorsha had indeed a mistrust for men. But a true hatred to commit such atrocities was undoubtedly caused by the gem in her chest. Thor stayed silent, and let Lexa carry on. "That was on the way here, I tried to get her alone to pull the gem from her chest but lost my opportunity. Took off on the ship when she attacked a small village. I half expect to see her flying overhead with her army at any moment."

Thor looked up. Then to Lexa's winged horse. "She made more of them?"

"All Cap Canna had to offer," Lexa replied. "She wants the world, Thor. All of it."

"We're in trouble," Thor said, looking at the stone floor of the balcony. "Raich is in trouble." He jumped down from the rail to stare the King in the eye. "She tell you of the wolves at Cherteri?" Cinna nodded. "Well, the wolves she spoke of. They've taken Tenzin. Its people are most likely all wolves now. And I'm betting they're on their way here as we speak. Gather all the silver you can to the armoury and start forging weapons, ready your guards, all the men of Raich…and the women. Put slings in the hands of children if you have to." The conversation finished in his mind, Thor turned and made for the stairs at the other end of Cinna's chambers.

Lexa followed.

"Ah, and what about you?" asked the king with wide eyes.

"If we're going to stand a chance, we're going to need the world's greatest tactician. I'll fetch him. He'll take charge of your defenses from here on out." Thor commanded the king.

"Wait. What?"—Lexa grabbed Thor's arm—"Lucius is *alive*, and *here*?"

Thor pushed open the doors, walked through leaving Cinna alone with a dumbfounded look upon his face. "It's best we go over everything once we reach the ship. Just hope he's got his wits about him."

"What ship? Whose wits? Lucius's?"

"The ship with the wagon full of gold…from Cherteri." Thor whispered.

Lexa nodded. "And what of Lucius's wits?"

"We have a lot to discuss about that. But that can wait." Thor held out his palm motioning for Lexa to lead the way down the stairs from the king's chambers. He was an abrupt, straight-to-the-point man, but he saw no sense in hitting Lexa with everything at once. He knew where her heart laid, and what she wanted to do; what she needed to do. "You have some reuniting to do. Take your mount, ships at the docks, I'll meet you there. And…I'll take the long way." He winked.

Her eyes watered again, and she let a grin slip. "See that you do."

Lexa raced down the stairs. Thor followed, but she had already taken to the air when he reached the courtyard. He aimed to give her and his cousin the reunion they needed. If Lucius was still out, they would have it.

Three comely maids passed him on the way out the gates, each donned in tight revealing clothes draped with robes of silk. Sisters he guessed by their resemblance to each other. He couldn't help himself. "I'm new to town, and thirsty. Do either of you know where a man can find a good cup of wine…you know…a place to meet his needs."

They giggled, as he'd found women do among themselves. The one he took for the eldest of the three stepped closer and spoke for them all. "We know of such a place." She put a hand on her hip, stepped closer to Thor, and ran a finger over his breastplate. "But are you enough man to keep up with the three of us?" She stood up straight heaving her chest skyward, stretching her tight ornately laced garb near to its breaking point.

Thor weighed his options. Life *was* an adventure. Wolves were approaching in numbers. Sorsha was most likely headed their way. Preparations needed to be made for both. On the other hand Lexa needed at least a turn of a glass with Eric, and Thor swore he'd take the long way back to the ship. He grinned at the comely women before him. He'd found that in moments such as this, it's best to not say something of little wit or too much excitement. "I like a challenge." But sometimes, confidence prevails.

~*~

Lexa's heart pounded faster with every beat of her horse's wings. Whether it be the excitement of knowing Lucius was alive and could possibly be their best chance at stopping Sorsha, the anticipation of seeing Eric again after thinking him dead, or a combination of both she didn't know. One thing was for sure, the closer to the docks she went, the stronger the butterflies churning in her stomach became.

It wasn't until she set eyes on the deck of the ship from Cherteri that she knew the answer. Her eyes watered once more as they had back on the balcony, and the stairway. Her horse thudded on the deck as she leapt clear of it and ran forward.

"What the—" Were the only words Eric got out before she toppled him to the deck.

Pressing her lips to his, she kissed him like no other she'd kissed before. The warmth of his body pressed against hers, along with his embrace, helped her forget where they were and what they were up against. Lexa ran her fingers through his short-cropped hair and pulled back to gaze into his dark brown eyes that always seemed to hold such mystery. "Don't ever do that again," she said.

"I think we should do that more often." Replied Eric in his normal jesting manner.

Lexa kissed him again, then sat up on top of him. "You know what I mean."

"What?" Eric shrugged. "If anyone should be mad, it's me. You pretending to be dead at Xanatos' cave and all. Tricking me so I'd change and save the day. Though it did work out." Eric furrowed his brow and broke eye contact with her for the first time since she'd set foot on deck. Then staring back up at her. "Then you had the nerve to make me worry while you went traipsing all over the world with Sorsha, of all people. I was beginning to think you were using me for my body."

Lexa ran her hand over his chest and let the memory of their nights together outweigh Eric's words until he opened his mouth again.

"Guess someone this handsome is just too hard to stay away from, eh?" He grinned larger than she'd ever seen before.

Lexa hit him in the gut with her palm as she stood up, forcing the air from his belly. She was about to retort, begin the natural banter that they share, but she caught movement out of the corner of her eye.

"Still full of himself, is he?" Lucius said, coming up the steps from the hold.

"*You*…I'm happy to see." Lexa stepped over Eric letting her foot hit him in the ribs as she went.

"Hey," Eric complained, though she knew neither her jab nor her kick had done Eric any harm.

Ignoring him, Lexa wrapped her arms around Lucius. "Thought you were all dead. I missed you more than you'll know."

Lucius craned his neck, looked over Lexa's shoulder, and said loud enough for Eric to hear. "Missed me more than the rest of the crew, isn't that sweet, darlin." Then softer, he whispered in her ear. "It's good to see you're all right. And don't let him fool you, his heart broke when he thought you were gone. And under that brash exterior, he's leaping for joy on the inside."

"I know." Lexa broke their embrace and stepped back.

"Going to bed them both?" Came a woman's voice from behind.

A voice Lexa thought could only belong to one person, a sultry yet timid voice turned to steel. "Darla." Lexa turned around to find Raven's lackey holding the tip of a sword to the throat of the man she just got back from the beyond.

Chapter Fourteen

Thor peered over the rail of the ship from the foot walk, pausing to see if Lexa and Eric required a lengthier period without interruption. Instead, he found Lexa beside Lucius, and Eric on the flat of his back with a dark-haired woman holding a blade to his throat. Thor drew his broadsword yet held back from charging onto the deck. The woman's stance, her command of a blade, drew familiarity to him. This woman held herself like a seasoned warrior. Sorsha's prowess in battle flashed through his mind. The woman, too short to be Sorsha, must be one from Cap Canna that Lexa spoke of. She was in no rush. Many seasons and countless battles had taught him that. This woman intended to intimidate, to toy with her victim before striking a killing blow. A quick glance of the board-walk and docks told him the woman was alone, a scout perhaps.

Could Sorsha know *they* were alive? Doubtful, they'd headed in opposite directions. Lexa, yes. This woman could be here for Lexa, so why hold a blade to Eric's throat? Though muffled, her voice was somewhat familiar to him as well. He'd have to strip her of her sword, and any other concealed blades, without killing her if he's to discover who she is, and more importantly why she was here.

All this went through his mind in a flash, questions that would have to wait to be answered later. Thor slipped on board and crept up behind the woman just beyond striking range. "Heh-em." Thor cleared his throat, stopping the woman from continuing her speech of betrayal that he wasn't paying attention to.

The blade at Eric's throat whirled around to pass between Thor and the mystery woman as she crouched to slice Thor's gut open. He was right to leave a gap between them, one which he had to make larger by jumping back to avoid the blow. One which he closed the moment the blade passed by.

His free hand took hold of her sword arm at the wrist while he put his shoulder into the woman's ample bosom. She tripped over Eric still sprawled on the deck to land beside him, weaponless.

"That's enough of that." Thor said, noting that the skills of Sorsha may have been passed to this woman, but the muscles trained to use and wield those skills had not.

"Mongrel dog." The woman rolled back, pulling out a dagger concealed beneath her robes.

"You sound like her too, but you're no warrior like her." Thor stepped over Eric, holding his sword out level to the deck. The mass of hair draped over her face obscured her identity. She lunged at him with the dagger. He batted it aside. She feinted a kick to the groin. A move Thor instinctively made to fend off, feinted or not, and exposed his chest for a strike. He lurched back as her blade skirted along his breastplate. The slender figure before him was not to be underestimated, and he aimed to end this dance, with a single blow. His kick to the gut dropped her to the deck. Lexa's kick flung the woman's dagger from her grasp.

"Stand down"—Thor stepped forward—"I don't wish to harm you."

"Son of a goat lover." Croaked the woman trying to force the air back inside her.

"There's that sharp tongue again."

"Maybe you shouldn't press her any further, cousin." Eric stood beside him.

"She was making to open your throat when I arrived. Now you want me to—"

"Thor?" the woman said, looking up at him, brushing her hair from her face. "It *is* you. Figures you've forgotten me already. Probably bedded Lady Lexa here along with any others on the ship. Treasonous harlot." She spat at Lexa's feet.

"Darla." Though he'd only spent a single night with her, and a memorable morning, Thor recognized her immediately without her hair covering her face. "You made it out of Cherteri after all. And...went...strait for Cap Canna"—Thor sighed—"Where she tainted you."

"Tainted. Tainted! I'll show you tainted you unfaithful lying sack of dung." Darla leapt, clawing for his face, disregarding all battle skills and leaving herself vulnerable. Thor dropped his sword, caught her by the wrists, spun her, weaving her arms around and over her head, restraining her, pinning her back against his chest in his embrace.

"Relax," Thor said in as calm a voice as he could muster. Knowing if Sorsha's influence had taken control of Darla's mind that any aggression would be returned ten-fold. "You're not yourself."

Darla struggled in vain beneath Thor's iron grip. "I'll have your head for that. You'll roast like the pig you are. Mark my words, you'll roast."

"I've had enough of this." Lexa drove her fist into Darla's jaw, knocking her out cold to fall limp in Thor's arms. "Needed to be done." She rubbed her knuckles. "Let her cool down, she might be manageable then. But now you see the grip Sorsha has on her, on all of them. That's what we're up against. An army of irrational Sorsha's all battle trained."

"Don't say it." Lucius cautioned Eric.

"Say what?" replied Eric. "That Sorsha was irrational to begin with. I'd never say that."

"You wonder why she's got a hate-on for men." Lexa tapped Eric on the cheek.

"Hey, she hated Thor long before she ever met me. This is all *his* fault." Eric pointed a thumb to Thor.

Scooping Darla up in his arms, Thor shook his head at his cousin. He was right, but looking down at the comely Darla in his arms he didn't want to believe she might be too far gone to bring her back. "That rage was not Darla, nor that of Sorsha. That was the rage of the Raven. I've seen it once before at the Red Ox before she destroyed it and entombed Cherteri."

"Well, that's what Sorsha's like to deal with now, ready to snap at anything. I'm sorry." Lexa put a hand on Lucius's shoulder. "But she didn't hate *all* men, mainly just those two." Lexa smirked, nodding behind her.

"It's not our fault Sorsha's—"

"No, she's right," Thor said, cutting off his cousin. "If we ever have a chance at keeping Sorsha from going blood drunk. You and I best keep out of sight."

"I agree with you on that," Lexa said. "But before you two come up with any kind of a plan, you need to know what I do. And I need to know what happened, not just Sorsha's cryptic version. For instance…what do you mean Cherteri was entombed? What happened at the mountain? All I know is we were in the thick of battle, and everything went dark."

Thor saw it on her face, this was the first time since being on board that Lexa looked at Lucius, truly looked him over, and realized what had happened to him.

Lexa hesitated, then placed her hand on his pale cheek. "Oh, Lucius."

"There's a lot we need to discuss. You three get started, I'll take care of her." Thor didn't wait for a reply, instead he looked over Darla cradled in his arms as he headed to the ship's hold. None of them would ever be the same. Seeing how Sorsha, Raven, had corrupted Darla and put a seed of doubt that his oath would be impossible to fulfill. Part of it had already slipped from his grasp. The people of Cherteri would have perished by now from lack of drink and food. He had reunited Lexa with his cousin, but that paled in comparison to the task ahead. He wouldn't give up though, it wasn't in him to back down. He had to hope that removing the gem in Sorsha's chest could restore her back to herself. Give Lucius back what was taken from him. Strip his cousin of his furry side. And now, as if his list wasn't long enough, he had to hope that the woman in his arms could once again become the one he knew. The one with wit, with a softness not only in her hands but in her eyes, the exact opposite of who he'd just grappled with.

He stepped below deck, letting his trio of companions share with each other what they knew, then laid Darla down on a pile of hides stacked against the hull, sat beside her, waited, and hoped.

Chapter Fifteen

"There's water beside you," Thor said in a soft voice to Darla opening her eyes, blinking as she took in her surroundings. "We're in the ship's hold."

"You don't think I'd recognize a ship's hold when I see one?"

That was Sorsha's tone talking again, Darla just missed adding the insult Sorsha would have.

"Thick-headed mound of muscle, good for pulling a wagon is about as useful as you are," Darla added, sitting up.

There it is, that sharp tongue Thor had come to know only too well. It didn't fit the beauty sitting before him. He'd spent enough time with Sorsha that he knew how to get her riled up, and thankfully, how not to. "You're right, But I'm also good at fetching things, like the waterskin beside you."

"Not good enough for a cup?" Darla swiped the waterskin from the hide she sat on.

Thor let her take a good long drink before he spoke of what he'd thought about while Darla slumbered. He knew he must try to get through to her, and not rouse Sorsha's influence. "Good to see you," he said as she pulled the waterskin from her lips.

"Suppose you've been eying me while I was out." Darla looked down at herself. "Surprised I'm still clothed."

There it is, his opportunity he thought. "It's true, last we were together you wore considerably less, as did I. If I recall correctly, it was you who undressed me. What a fortunate man I am." Thor ran his finger along the table top he sat at, staring at it, doing his best to look patient, yet like a man deep in thought, hoping she'd follow his lead and not only recall their time together, but the feelings he stirred in her when she was free of Raven's influence.

"*Were.*" Darla corrected him, getting to her feet with her voice becoming elevated. "You *were* a fortunate man to have lain with me. Don't you *dare* think it'll happen again."

"I shall try to satisfy you." Thor raised his head, looked her in the eyes, searched to see if she recalled the last conversation they had together in their bed-chamber back in Cherteri. One where they teased each other, bantered back and forth, about satisfying each others hunger. A hunger for each other's embrace.

Darla stopped in mid-step toward him, as if something he'd said had reached her. The true her that he had come to know, albeit so briefly. He waited for what seemed like a lifetime as Darla just stared at him. Her eyes softened, glared a little less, told him there was a passion growing behind them. Be that for his companionship or his death he didn't know.

Darla rested a fist on her hip. "Satisfy me?" She paused, as if reminiscing, then a grin set in on her lips. "That's the way it should be. With *me* telling you what *I* like. What *I* want. What I *need.* And you—"

"Shall fulfill your every request." Thor cut her off before she could sling an insult his way just as Sorsha would have, a risk worth taking.

Darla bit her bottom lip and let it slide between her teeth as she looked him over. "Stand up."

Darla spoke as if she was giving him a command, though Thor thought her voice had softened, not by much, but enough to detect. He held his tongue, stood from the table.

"Take off your clothes."

Once again, Thor complied without a word.

~*~

Footsteps coming from above deck along with the evening sun's rays shining through the portholes told Thor just how long he'd been down in the hold. The warmth of Darla's naked body pressed against his beneath the furry hide kept the chill of the coming night at bay. His bare shoulder felt the chill only being around flowing water can bring. His other shoulder was warm as can be, thanks to Darla's head resting on it.

"I could stay here forever." She turned to rest her chin on his chest and look him in the eye.

"Whatever satisfies you." Thor grinned.

She traced a line with her finger on his chest. "Thank you."

"For what?"

"For finding me."

Indeed, Thor thought he had. Their embrace had begun forceful, with Darla acting how Thor guessed Sorsha would, but as he gave into her, something in her shifted, softened, and she bedded him as she had before, talented, but with not a hint of the hostility she began their dance with.

"I no longer feel…*her*…anymore."

"It was my pleasure. I knew I was good, but—" Darla pinched his ribs, prodding him to cut his words short and jerk from her touch.

"You're good, but not *that* good. You reached me"—she rested her palm on her chest—"here."

"I stopped listening after *you're good.*" Thor smirked.

"Get up," Darla said, pushing him from beneath the hide to the floor, then wrapped the hide around her. "I want some food."

Thor folded his hands behind his head and winked at her as he lay on the cold planks, nude. "You sure that's all?"

She tossed the hide in his face as she rose.

He admired her, for a moment, memorizing the shadows shifting over her as she collected her garb. She answered his question with silence, so he followed her lead, donning his breeches, boots and shirt. He pulled on his breastplate, leaving Darla to do whatever it is that takes women so long to get dressed in peace, and went above deck. Eric smirked at him, gently bobbing his head up and down, prompting an elbow to the ribs from Lexa. Lucius, however, had a look of concern about him.

"What troubles you?" Thor asked.

"Aside from Lexa confirming what you said Sorsha has become, and then some?" replied Lucius. "Just the fact that we're about to fight a battle on two fronts, and I'm pretty sure we're all gonna die."

"Pretty sure?"

"I was trying to be optimistic."

"Optimism is good but it won't help against Raven," Darla said, coming up from the hold. Lucius frowned, eyeing her. Eric and Lexa stood from the rail they were leaning against, neither going for a blade, but both standing at the ready. "I'm not mad anymore, if that's what you're thinking." Darla drummed her fingers on Thor's breastplate. "He helped with that."

She kissed him on the cheek, then swayed her hips as she made her way to the steps leading to the stern. Thor grinned, thought about letting that be the end of it as his companions looked at him with questions brewing behind their eyes, aside from Eric repeating his head bobbing. Thor shifted his gaze between Lucius and Lexa. He pointed to where Darla had stroked his breastplate, then tapped his temple. Lucius, always quick of wit, was the first of them to look back at Darla, though it seemed to Thor that more questions were forming under the man's cap. Lexa jabbed Eric again stifling his childish antics that Thor was accustomed to, then she sent him a grin, rubbing the back of her neck as if forming the same notion as he had as she blushed at his cousin.

If he could free Darla from Raven's hold, and Lexa could free Eric's mind from the wolf's hold, then surely Lucius could do the same for Sorsha.

Plopping herself down to lounge on the steps leading to the stern Darla pulled the cork from a wine jug and took a drink. "Quite the selection you guys brought."

"She's got the right idea." Lucius turned, went to the hold.

"I know you from the Feisty Goat, don't I?" Darla pointed her wine jug. "Eric, right?"

"Hang on, Lucius," Eric said, ignoring Darla's question and scurrying after Lucius. "I'll give you a hand at selecting a good vintage."

"It's my wine, I know what's the best." Lucius frowned at Eric rushing to his side.

Eric paused. "Right." He waved his hand gesturing for Lucius to make haste. "Just go."

Thor studied his cousin, his awkward display. Thor met Darla at the Feisty Goat, and Eric had procured a room at the Feisty Goat there for a few moons before Thor had arrived in Cherteri. Darla earned coin there as a serving maid. That's where Thor met her, he had no doubt Eric knew her. She knew him. Whether it was from a bedding or an event that made Eric's cheeks redden, Thor didn't know. Eric's embarrassed, but Darla doesn't seem to be. Thor wanted to know what it was that happened between the two of them. Not so much because he cared how they knew each other, or what they did, but so he could exploit his cousin's embarrassment, poke a jab or two at him; like they always do. The truth would come out, of that Thor was certain, wine had a truth-telling brewed into it, and he looked forward to it.

Darla grinned at Eric's back, then abandoned her one-sided conversation with Eric and turned to Lexa. "What's your story, when you're not helping Raven take over the world and knocking me cold? Good one by the way." Darla rubbed her jaw.

"Sorry, but you weren't being very reasonable," replied Lexa, to which Darla rolled her eyes. "I know she had control over you. What I want to know is how she doesn't anymore."

"Well, you see, all it takes is—"

"Shut it." Darla tossed the cork at Thor, silencing him from answering Lexa for her. "It *was* him, but not in the way *he'd* have you believe. He…touched me"—Darla rested her hand over her chest—"reminded me of who I was…before meeting Raven." She dropped her gaze to the ship's deck. "Maybe being so far from her helped too, less influence, I don't know. But it was a revival of old feelings that still stirred within me that brought me back from…whatever."

Thor grinned, couldn't restrain himself. "I think your recovery was also due to physical exhaustion."

Darla looked up, swatted the air in his direction.

Lexa laughed. "No man's that good."

"If he could lessen her burden, relax her mind for her," Eric said with a smug look on his face, accepting one of the four bottles of wine Lucius carried and held it out for Lexa. "I could do the same for you if you need."

"They're not related at all, are they?" Darla shook her head, addressing Lexa.

Lexa smiled, swiped the bottle from Eric's grasp. "Women and wine. Two obsessions every man craves and boasts about." Lexa sat beside Darla, leaned a shoulder against hers. "Boasts which more often than not aren't entirely accurate."

"Too true." Darla grinned at Lexa, took a pull of wine, then stared at Thor. "Sometimes it's best they just keep their mouths shut."

Thor wasn't one to back down from a battle of playful, jabbing, conversation. Not due to Darla's suggestion, but because Darla's mind had just been freed of Raven's influence, and Thor didn't want to push her too hard too fast. He considered remaining silent and letting the women continue their banter and bashing without interruption. He accepted a bottle from Lucius. On the other hand there was work to be done, and plans to make.

"What matters is that you're free, and if repeating past indulgences freed you from Raven's grasp" —Thor kept a straight face—"then perhaps the same can be said for Sorsha," Thor said, looking from Darla to Lucius.

"Yeah, I get it, the worlds depending on me." Lucius slumped down against the mast.

"No different than any other day," Eric said, hopping up to sit on the deck's rail.

"No pressure." Lucius added, taking a long haul on his bottle, looking defeated.

"None whatsoever." Eric hoisted his bottle, then swirled the wine inside as he studied it. "Didn't you once say that with enough time you could prepare for any foe? Well, here's another chance to prove it again just as you did at Cherteri building the city's defenses, not to mention devising how to empty the king's coffers. Course that's only because Lexa and I let you take the credit."

Lucius huffed at Eric's attempt to raise his spirits, but his composure didn't change.

"We've got what...two nights at best before we're in the thick of battle with *his* kin?" Thor pointed at Eric who shrugged his shoulder and leaned to his side, lounging on the rail, supporting his weight on his elbow. "Even if Sorsha's building an army, and if she brings it to us we'll be better prepared than if we have to bring the fight to her. We took down Xanatos, his winged wolf, and an army of creatures sent our way. This time we're not fighting the king as well; we have a cooperative king and an entire city with us. You should be excited to scribble plans in your book for our defenses."

Eric chuckled. "If you haven't drawn them up already that is." He stretched out, laying on the rail, gazing at the sky. "I got a few ideas."

"It's not that." Lucius scratched at the top of his wine bottle with his finger.

"What then?" Thor took a sip of wine, waited for an answer as opposed to prodding his friend further.

Lexa stood from beside Darla and rested a hand on Thor's shoulder, silencing him as she walked over to Lucius. She squatted, looked him in the eye. "Don't worry, she still does."

"I hope you're right." Lucius dropped his gaze, started tapping the bottom of his wine bottle against the deck.

"Who does what now?" Eric asked, still gazing skyward.

Thor felt the same as his cousin. Lexa appeared to have picked up on whatever it is that had Lucius concerned.

"Definitely related." Lexa stood, shook her head at Thor then slid her finger along Eric's arm as she passed him by.

Lucius grinned. He didn't miss a beat in his cryptic conversation with Lexa. Lucius was, for the most part, a confident man. Perhaps it was his task of saving Sorsha the same way Thor had saved Darla that troubled him. Thor swished the sweet wine in his mouth, tracking Lexa as she crossed the deck slightly shaking her head. Lexa picked up her bottle, sat beside Darla, and whispered something in her ear.

"Sometimes they're not even good for that." Darla hoisted her jug, agreeing with whatever Lexa said.

Lexa clinked her bottle off of Darla's jug, pointed a finger at Thor and then Eric, wagging it.

"Whispers are lies." Eric sat up, pointed back at Lexa, and then shifted his attention to Lucius. "And they don't need any encouragement from you."

Thor nodded his agreement with his cousin.

Darla chuckled, slapped a hand on Lexa's knee. "Oh, are they ever related."

"Can we get on with a plan of attack, or defence, or something before the two of you hurl more insults at us without actually speaking to us."

"Agreed," Thor said.

Lucius stood from the mast, nodded to the women. "Tonight, we drink as if its the last night we'll ever see each other. Because as of tomorrow, we part ways, all of us." He climbed the steps to the stern, rummaged around in a barrel. Whatever was bothering Lucius, he appeared to be over it, or at the least was masking his discomfort. That suited Thor fine. The man was intelligent, and would work out the issue. More importantly the conversation shifted away from him and Eric.

"Last night we'll see each other. Nice. Guy knows how to put a damper on things." Thor caught Darla say about Lucius, quietly to Lexa.

"Not usually." Lexa leaned forward, resting her elbows on her knees.

Lucius came down the steps with a sack in his hands, heavy enough he leaned to one side. He tossed it, spilling gold coins across the deck. "Anti up. Best story wins the pot."

"Ohhh, I'm gonna win." Eric dashed off, started rummaging in the same barrel.

"How's that?" Thor called to Eric's back. "I'm the one who makes all your stories great."

Lucius turned to the women, took a breath and stood tall. "They're not gonna win."

"Neither are you," Darla and Lexa said in unison.

Chapter Sixteen

"There's no way her story's better than mine. I mean come on, not a single mention of a tavern," Eric complained.

Lexa padded her pile of gold coins that dwarfed those of the others. "You're just jealous we've each won a hand except for you. Some of more than once." Lexa grinned. "I can't help it that I lived more in my first 12 summers than you have to this very moment."

Eric shook his head. "Enjoy that pile while you can, because you'll be looking at it from way over there when its by my side."

"Well yeah, after cleaning you out of your share, I'll have to pay you to carry all *my* gold."

"Ohh, I like that." Darla rolled a gold coin across the table to Eric. "I get him first." She winked at Lexa.

"Now ladies"—Lucius interrupted before Lexa could throw another jab Eric's way—"it's not that our dear friend here hasn't any good stories, he merely lacks the skill to tell them in a manner that will appeal to more than children. And apologies, Lexa, I will be the second to put his back to work carrying my share of his gold." Lucius slid a coin across the table to Eric's meager pile."

"Told you, cousin, the best part of your stories is me. Next bet, why don't you tell them how I saved you from that bear with nothing but a rope," Thor smirked.

"It was a cub."

"So were you."

Eric had just about had enough of his companion's prodding. Part of him, a small part, believed he deserved it after bragging he'd have the biggest pile. Though, he was picking up on an alliance forming, one comprised of everyone but him.

"I've got a better one that involves you, since you're so fond of thinking my tales a naught without you cousin. Remember when you had to run through my village, naked? Trying to get away from the Vallin sisters' older brother. Yep, you were quite the warrior that night. Pretty sure—" Eric paused, craned his neck to the west. Listened over the creaking of the ship lulling in the river. Louder than the waves licking the ships hull, louder than the buzz of the taverns on the boardwalk, Eric picked out the snarl of a wolf, one not from nature. He looked up at the crescent moon illuminating the scattered clouds above. Was he more attune at night, to the wolves? No one else had heard a thing. Had he spent so many nights thieving, lurking in the shadows, that the darkness spoke to him? His heart sped. "You hear that?"

"What? The sound of you going broke?" Lexa jested.

"No." Eric stood from the table, spilling his meager pile of gold to the deck, ignoring it. He needn't see his companions faces; he knew his lack of action to the gold alone told them to stand at the ready. Thor loosed his blade, stood abreast of him. Lucius snapped his steel bow into place, nocked an arrow. "Out there, by that farm house beyond the boardwalk, sounded like…a wolf."

A scream cut through the night, overtaking the argues drone of Raich.

"It's too dark, can't see anything beyond the boardwalk's lanterns." Thor stepped to the rail squinting.

"They're here already? It's too soon. You said we had time."

Darla spoke to all of them, and yet none of them. Any trace of Sorsha's rage, control, had been removed from Darla, even her instincts, Eric thought. At the moment, he hoped Sorsha's hardened battle skills remained. Another cry sounded, closer. The people of Raich loitering on the boardwalk ceased what they were doing. The constant buzz creeping out of the most westerly taverns died.

"My leg is not annoyed any more than it is with just the two of you around." Lucius shook his leg, testing it. "They could not have made it here from Tenzin so soon, could they? When we were there, it felt as if it would burn off, felt like I would be left with naught but a nub below the knee."

"Scouts," Thor said.

"Sent by the pack?" Lexa turned from the west, from the others, peering into the night across the river. "You really think they're that organized."

Eric shut his eyes, concentrated, reached out with his palm, reached out with his…furry self. "They're more like rogues." He couldn't see them in his mind, but he felt them, sensed their presence. Not like a wave of mindless creatures cresting the horizon, more like scattered solitary beasts anticipating a meal. "In search of food."

"Food? You mean us?" Darla took hold of Thor's forearm, looked over her shoulder. "We'll never make the city walls. Pull the anchor…float away…that'll work."

"We'll survive them as long as it's not the full force," Thor said, attempting to comfort her.

Eric looked over the pair, desperation filled Darla, her poise, her voice, her eyes. It struck him, though Sorsha was a fierce warrior, Darla may have never seen battle, or even been in a fight for that matter, and if she was truly free of Raven's grasp then she'd be in his cousin's charge, clinging to his shadow, hindering movement.

"How many you wager there are, cousin?"

Eric reached out again, eyeing the buildings on the horizon. "Four…no there's another one, calmer than the others, less blood lust. It's hunting, but not for food, it's searching." He was one of them, attached to their minds. He could sense them, and they could possibly sense him. Part of the pack, he thought. It became harder to swallow, felt as if even the cool mist of the river wouldn't moisten his lips. He hated the idea of becoming one of them, again. The power was undeniable, but the lack of control was terrifying, especially being so close to his companions.

"Where?" Lexa shielded her eyes from the light of the ship, of the city, still searching.

"Its not like looking through a window, just a feeling, kind of like how you know which way the wind comes from when your eyes are closed."

"Well start using your eyes." Thor calmly removed Darla's grasp on his arm, made for the foot walk. "The guards don't have silver weapons like the Elite from Cherteri did, let alone the people. Lucius, put some arrows in that thing."

A wolf had made the boardwalk, slashed open the gut of a man stumbling out of a tavern.

Thor let out a battle cry, charged toward it, sword held high overhead. Tavern patrons fleeing the wolf parted before him, closed the gap behind him, hindering Eric's pursuit. Out of range of his arrows, Lucius followed, bogged down worse than Eric by the people. His cousin always strived for adventure and battle, but taking the wolf head-on could get him killed, especially when Lucius has silver arrows. Course, Thor can heal like he can, but can he do it fast enough if need be? Eric's sword sang as he pulled it free of its scabbard, not made of silver it could only inflict wounds that would heal.

Hopefully, with his enhanced speed and strength, he could follow.

The wolf snarled. Thor leapt, roared, dropped his broadsword, and continued past the howling beast, skidding to a halt.

Eric closed the gap, emerged from the crowd, saw the damage his cousin inflicted. The wolf, howling, yelping, clutched at its severed forearm. He felt its pain, felt sympathy for it. Eric shook the notion from his mind as the creature spun around after Thor, its blood lust overpowering any instinct to cradle the spurting stump spraying the boardwalk.

As fast as Thor was, he couldn't match the creature's speed. Eric, unable to stop it, watched the wolf rake its claws down his cousin's back, rendering strips of leather from his breastplate, and flesh from bone. Thor collapsed to his knees.

"No!" Eric shouted, forgoing all tactics at the sight of his cousin torn open. He ran all out holding his sword like a lance at the creature's chest. The wolf batted the blade aside, and Eric slammed his shoulder into its gut.

They tumbled over each other, the back of Eric's thigh screamed at him, slashed open. His sword lost, he grunted, not just from the pain, but from the frustration of the beast inside him, trying to claw its way out. The wolf came up on top of their wrestling match. Eric grasped its throat, locked his elbow, holding snapping fangs at bay. "Enough!" he yelled, driving his fist into its furry jaw.

His chest burned, from the inside, he was about to change if he couldn't keep his wits about him.

"Not now. Stop. Stop it!" he shouted to himself more than the wolf.

Sinew and muscle beneath his fingers relaxed. The wolf in his grasp breathed as heavy as he, yet didn't move. Eric focused, tried to clear the crimson hue overtaking his vision, see past his other side and realized he did it, he stopped the wolf with nothing more than his words. The burning rage in his chest diminished, and the beast inside him skulked back. For what seemed like a turn of the glass he stared at the wolf, and it back at him. Both studying each other, neither knowing what to make of their unusual bond.

A shaft in the eye sprayed lifeblood from the wolf, breaking their bond, killing it instantly. Eric shoved its corpse to the side. Lucius stood atop a barrel, above the crowd, poised with his bow in his hand, its string still vibrating from letting loose its payload.

Howls sounded in the distance, followed by yelps. Eric reached out again, felt pain, felt death. Lucius, another arrow notched, didn't raise his bow. He nodded. From his vantage point, Lucius would be able to see what Eric felt, the people of Raich slaying the remaining rogue wolves. No longer able to sense a single wolf, Eric turned to his cousin.

Thor, on hands and knees, coughed, spit blood, fingered his back, and his slashed open breastplate. "Well, that was fun."

Eric dropped his head to the boardwalk. "Fun?"

"Another tale with me in it for you to tell."

"Nice to see you're feeling better, but next time, we do it together."

"If you can keep up." Thor stood, arched his back.

Eric just shook his head at his cousin. Even before Thor had…changed, been able to heal, he could hold his own in battle. The wounds he suffered tonight were obviously on the mend, and wouldn't have been fatal due to his cousin's mindset. A way of thinking, one that no doubt has saved his life numerous times in the past. The hardened leather breastplate he always donned, along with its multiple battle scars was testament to that. But if they were to take on the army of wolves from Tenzin, he feared they would need to be even more diligent than Thor ever was. Then it came to him, a possible solution. The question was, could Eric and his other self pull it off? Could he command the pack?

Chapter Seventeen

"You want to do *what?*" King Cinna stopped his inspection of the city's wall.

"Empty your coffers," Lucius repeated, squinting from the morning sun in his eyes as they strolled alongside the city's wall.

It never ceased to amaze Lucius, how it took many turns of the glass to convince a king to empty his purse.

"Buy all the silver in the city if you have to." Lucius continued. "I do not care if you have to trade every man woman and child equal weight in gold to get it. Because if you do not, there might not be a city left standing."

"My coffers aren't that of King Isaks." King Cinna shook his head, a look of dread on his face.

"Then convince the people to give it to you." Thor ran his fingers along the wall's crumbling mortar. "You saw the remnants of last night's attack, the heavy losses. Five wolves, twenty-four men. Drunkard, mercenary, guard, they didn't stand a chance without silver."

"Let's say we use all my silver, and the peoples, then what? Coat blades and arrows in silver like you've said you did. Won't make much of a difference unless we coat pitch forks. Most of the people around you are farmers and merchants, not soldiers." King Cinna gestured to the people roaming the streets around them.

Lucius turned from King Cinna, bent to inspect one of the city's catapults. "I plan to fix it so they will not need to be soldiers. Besides, there are not enough turns of the glass for proper instruction. Arm everyone, those skilled with a sword, coat their blades, along with every arrowhead in the city. But the common folk, they are going to operate these. "Ideally, I'd like to have a full score of catapults to the north for Sorsha's army, and another to the west for the wolves. Not the dozen or so you have scattered around the city."

"When's the last time they've been fired?" Eric flicked the catapult's support. "Looks like they'll tear themselves to pieces."

"We will fix them if needed." Lucius waved his hand, dismissing the thought, continued on to the next catapult. "Just get every one of them you have to the north and west walls. Test their distances and mark each one."

Cinna nodded to one of the five guards following them, issuing a silent command to fulfill Lucius's wishes. The guard left, though in no rush, Lucius noted.

"Test them with stones weighted the same," Lucius called to the guards back, a hand wave told him he got the message.

A coal fire fume wafting from heated metal caught Lucius's attention. He stood before the open tent, digging in his purse. Since his raid in Cherteri, and emptying King Isak's coffers of gold, silver had become rare. Finding a piece, his last one, he tossed the coin to the burly smith. "Can you put that to the grinding wheel and work it into a dust?"

The smith looked at Lucius with a puzzled look then shrugged his shoulders. "Waste of coin if you ask me." He turned to the grinding wheel. His foot working the pedal spinning the large round stone before him. Sparks flew from the coin into a clay bowl he placed under the grindstone.

"Not going to melt it down?" Thor asked as sparks shot from the coin into a clay bowl.

"Not all of it, if this works." Lucius leaned to see the bowl's contents. "That's good enough." He set a gold coin on the table as payment, receiving a wide-eyed look of shock from the smith. "Eric, your hand."

Eric tilted his head to the side, frowning. "Really?"

"I have to know if this will work." Lucius tapped the silver shards in the bowl with his finger, ensuring they were cool to the touch. Eric, frowning, held out his hand for Lucius's test. He raised the bowl to his face. "Do *not* breathe in." With a nod from Eric, he blew the shards over the back of his hand.

Eric grunted, gritted his teeth, yet held his hand in place. His skin spackled in red burn marks where every silver speck landed. Though he knew his friend was in pain, Lucius had to be certain, not of the silver, but the fact that any amount could produce a reaction, no matter the size. "Clean yourself up."

"Satisfied?" Eric pulled his hand back and wiped it on his robe.

"Yep," Lucius nodded, somewhat engaged in the conversation, but mostly running scenarios through his mind as easily as if he were sketching an unheard-of weapon on parchment. "Think what that would do if you filled your chest with it, breathed it in." He turned to King Cinna, leaving Eric with a concerned look on his face as he studied the back of his hand. "We need more, a lot more, as fine as the smiths can make it. See that the powder is loaded into clay jars, then seal them, but only once they have been weighed, *on a balance scale*"—Lucius pointed at the king—"to match the stones the guards are testing at the western catapults."

"Burn them from the inside out." Thor pinched at the shards, rubbed them between his fingers. "Nice."

"Not really." Eric held his hand up.

"I can see why Isak employed you, master architect." King Cinna looked from Eric's burn to Lucius. "What else do you have in mind?"

"Plenty. The question is whether we have enough turns of the glass, and the resources to implement them all. We will start with the basics, that which is the most easily achieved. Line the wall with archers with silver-tipped arrowheads to the west, regular steel to the north. Weight jars of lantern oil to match the silver powder, make sure some are heavier as well. Mark them clearly, as well their distances. Stack them separately from the rest. When this goes down, there will not be time for confusion, your men will have to act on instinct, like an animal." Lucius winked at Eric.

"They *are* still people Lucius," Eric said.

"Not at night," Thor corrected his cousin.

Lucius chuckled, recalling how he first met Thor, shackled to the barracks floor in Cherteri. "Oh, we will have scouts out there. If our fortunes hold, perhaps we can capture them, contain them, in much more comfortable accommodations than you and I met in. If we can get to them before night falls, we might be able to contain this before it happens."

Thor shook his head, even as Lucius spoke. "Doubt even Cherteri had enough cells to contain this horde, we're talking the city of Tenzin here. All wolves. Even if there was room, what then? Hope none get out? That's too risky."

"I agree," King Cinna said. "We don't have room for such numbers. I just can't believe the people of Tenzin would want to come here; our two cities have always been at peace."

"It's not them, it's their other halves." Eric looked to the cobbles, ashamed. "They can't control it. It's like you turn blood-drunk. There's no controlling that urge. I wouldn't like the idea of spending every night in a cell, I doubt they would either."

Thor put his hand on Eric's shoulder. "Even if they turned back for Tenzin by day, to go back to their homes *they* burned down. Which I doubt they would. They're way faster at night as wolves, with only one thought in their heads. They need to be put down unless they can control their furry halves."

Seeing the torment in his friend, Lucius decided he would reason with him, try to comfort him, allow him to come to a conclusion that sits well on his shoulders. Even if that decision needs some prodding. "You are right, Eric, they are people, and in human form they can be reasoned with. But unless they can control themselves, which you do not even have a full hold of yet, we have no other choice but to prepare for battle. Of course, if you could refrain from giving into your primal urges and control them, as an alpha does in the wild, well that would be a different story."

"Control them?" King Cinna stepped forward.

"Still just a theory, if we could prove it like the powder here then that would change everything."

"I get it, I don't like it much, but I get it." Eric flexed his hand, rubbing the scarred burns off to reveal perfectly new skin.

"They can heal like that?" King Cinna nodded to Eric's hand.

"Um-hm." Lucius hummed. "But if they breathe it in, they can't wipe it off. Those that make it past the powder, which shouldn't be many, will find a wall of fire holding them at bay thanks to the lantern oil. Silver arrows will follow shortly after."

"What happens if they make it into my city?"

"Strait to phase two this time," Lucius said, strolling away from the entrance of the smith's tent. "What Cherteri's finest failed to implement."

"Light the nets." Thor nodded, mulling over Lucius's words.

"Exactly," Lucius pointed to him, then addressed King Cinna. "Tangle them in fire as they come over the wall. Have tipped spears at the ready, make sure your people keep their distance. Even wounded these things are deadly. If any slip past the spears, blades can cut them down. There won't be much left of the buildings outside the city walls, but the people can rebuild, if they are alive. Who knows, if some wolves are injured, and captured, they could live out their nights, caged, and their days as men, free to roam about. Learn how to control themselves." Lucius looked to Eric, ensuring his long-time drinking companion picked up that the last bit was meant for him, to lift his spirits. Eric's shifting eyes, scrunched mouth, told Lucius he was thinking about it, and if he did not speak against it—not a normal trait of Eric's to stay silent—then he was in agreeance.

"You speak like they're unstoppable then you talk of how to stop them all, not to mention burning my city down to the ground, like this is one big game for you, like this is the end of Raich, like—"

"It was for Cherteri." Thor Cut King Cinna's words short.

King Cinna, looked as if he was about to retort, but held himself back as three comely maids approached them, all dressed in matching lace. At first, Lucius took the king's reaction as a measure to keep silent, keep the people from knowing what is truly transpiring in a city. He'd seen it before, numerous times, and most recently at Cherteri when King Isak tried to hide Xanatos's existence.

"Good morning, my daughters." King Cinna held his arms wide, embracing the three maids, stifling any further conversation. He released his daughters and gestured to Lucius and his companions. These are the travellers from Cherteri I spoke of. The ones who've come to our aid. Lucius, Eric, and—"

"Thor," said the tallest of the three, interrupting her father.

King Cinna frowned, looked between the two.

Eric rubbed his temples, leaned closer to Lucius, spoke soft enough Lucius could barely hear him. "Ugh, it's the Valin sisters all over again."

Lucius had heard the cousin's jest about the Valin sisters, more than once. Though the exact details behind their encounter with them evaded him. He knew Thor had bedded both sisters, and their brother ran him out of the village. He found that hard to believe that any man could intimidate Thor. Though he was in his youth when he encountered the Valin sisters, Lucius suspected Thor would have been a warrior at any age. But if Thor had bedded one, two, or all three of Cinna's daughters, that could pose an issue. Lucius studied them, trying to decide if Thor had indeed complicated measures. Thor's lack of embarrassment, the women's lack of hatred or endearing looks toward him, and how only the pair of them that hadn't spoken yet were giggling told him all was well. But when it comes to matters of women, no man really knows what drives them.

"You left us so soon," The tallest daughter said to Thor, closing the distance between them "Never quenched your needs, I think."

King Cinna may not have picked up on it, but Lucius did. This maid, though a woman he guessed to have seen near thirty summers, was bold to infer a bedding with her father so close, or so he thought until he looked back to Cinna. One of his other daughters held his attention, turning his face toward hers, speaking softly so he'd have to strain the hear her. A well-practiced move on their part, Lucius thought.

"I—"

"Shhh,"—her back to her father, the lone sister pressed her finger against Thor's lips—"we forgive you. If—"

"If *what?*" Darla said, one hand on her hip, the other on her hilt.

Chapter Eighteen

For the second time in as many days Lucius caught a glimpse of Sorsha. Her stance, her persona, and her rage, all portrayed by Darla. It was the latter that troubled him the most. Sorsha's undeniable, near to the point of hatred, feelings toward Thor. It was that rage he saw in Darla as she glowered at King Cinna's daughter pawing Thor. Lucius contemplated his next move, his next words, that might be able to soften the glare on Darla's face, and stay her hand on her hilt. "Darla," he said, with as much enthusiasm as his voice could produce. "Just the woman I wanted to see. You have absolute perfect timing. We were just going over the defenses, and I would love to hear your take on them. Any suggestions?"

Darla stood ready to strike. Whether that be to skewer Thor, Cinna's daughter, or both, he wasn't sure.

She hesitated, then tore her gaze from her target, let out a low growl from her throat at him, then stepped forward, honing in on his one-time cell mate and the harlot before him.

Having the king's daughter cut down before him would not bode well for them. If his words could not stop Darla, he doubted he could disarm her if she truly bore Sorsha's skills. But perhaps his presence could be enough, he hoped. He stepped forward, positioning himself between the wood-be combatants.

Darla put a palm on his chest, pushing, though not quite a shove, but forceful enough to make Lucius step aside. "Go on," Darla demanded of Cinna's daughter, closing the distance to her, getting right in her face.

Words, that is all that would be exchanged, for the moment. Sorsha's forked tongue was about to lash out, and if Darla had some of Sorsha left in her, Lucius knew she was too close to draw her sword. He'd seen Sorsha in battle, fought beside her, knew all too well her prowess, her cunning, and her…skill with a blade. He darted his eyes about searching for a dagger that Darla surely had concealed if she was still anything like Sorsha.

Cinna's daughter backed from Thor, but not from Darla. "Back off—"

Darla slapped Cinna's daughter hard enough to turn the woman's head then pointed a finger in Thor's face. "He's spoken for."

Darla may have adopted some of Sorsha's traits, but she was herself, acting like a tavern maid, defending her patron from a harlot, nothing like a warrior, like Sorsha. If she had, she would have put her fist in the woman's nose, breaking it, and sending her to the cobbles. Lucius relaxed, knowing all he was about to witness would be a skirmish.

Cinna's daughter raised her palm, moved to hit Darla back when Thor moved between the two, caught her slap on his shoulder, followed by another from her other hand. "How dare you strike me? You know who I am?"

Thor restrained her, held her wrists. "A friend," he said, more to Darla than to the woman. Guiding her away from Darla he continued. "One who soon will be in the midst of a battle with *all* of us standing together."

Cinna's daughter struggled, but calmed. Darla raised her chin, smirking.

The king made to speak but was silenced by his other daughters holding him by the arms, shaking their heads. It didn't take much effort on their part. The eldest of the three was the one that caused the most ruckus, Lucius surmised.

Eric groaned. "Be smart, cousin."

"I don't believe this will turn out to be anything similar to the Valin sister's event you two speak of." Lucius leaned closed to Eric.

"Better not." Lexa, Lucius noted, her arms folded across her chest, but her one finger rested on something bulging beneath her robes. The pommel of one of her throwing knives, Lucius figured. "One sorcerer was enough to deal with. We can't have you two running around enticing those of high position to want to take our heads."

"That was him," Eric gestured at Thor, guiding the daughter further from Darla. "Not me."

"Yes, well I'm sure you had something to do with it." Lexa jabbed a finger in Eric's chest, strode past Darla, winking at her, and put a hand on Thor's shoulder. "Let go of her already before I throttle you." She nodded at Cinna's daughter, prompting a calmer, less furrowed brow on the woman's face. "All you men know is brute strength. Not like us women who have the resolve and wit to settle disputes with our words."

Thor released his hold, slowly turned to Lexa, yet said nothing.

"Forgive my companion here for being so brash." Lexa brushed Thor aside, held her hand out to the woman. "You know how we can be protective over our possessions, don't you…"?

Cinna's daughter eyed Darla, then Thor, then took Lexa's hand. "Lucia."

"Lexa."

"I understand that. But she had no right to strike me."

"I didn't even leave a mark." Darla defended herself before Lucia could say more.

"If you're quite finished," King Cinna said, stepping from his other daughters. "We should carry on."

Lucia dropped her gaze, nodded. Darla wrapped her arm around Thor's, murmured just loud enough for Lucius to catch. "We're not finished."

"Right you are, Cinna," Lexa said. "You all should prepare, and we should be setting sail so you can get to it, give you time. In the off chance we fail, you don't want Raich to end up like Cherteri."

"Yeah, about that." Eric rubbed the back of his neck. "We're...prepared...for the wolves." He sighed. "But what are we to do if Sorsha comes here, all Raven-like and not herself?"

Lucius knew where Eric was going. Slay all the wolves, which he feels responsible for. Then just try to save Sorsha without the chance of putting a blade to her, let alone her army. "If Darla is any indication, there might be hope for the women she controls. Though without their families to coax them back to sanity there may not be. But if separating Sorsha from the stone can free her, it might do the same for the women she commands. If our fortune's hold, even turn the men and children back to normal."

"Doubt that. Freeing a mind is one thing, but changing a pig back into a man. I don't know...sorcery." Thor spat.

"I agree." Darla pulled back from Thor, nodding at his gesture. "Sorcery is something that's...unpredictable."

Lucius thought he caught something in her tone, as if she was withholding something, something embarrassing. He let it slide, there would be enough time on the ship to discover anything he needed to. "Regardless, we have to try. And if we fail"—Lucius was now the one dropping his head—"she's already lost to us."

He turned, continued their route to the city gates. The others made to follow him save for Cinna's daughters. No one spoke for the next few paces; Lucius could feel the tension as he was sure his companions were looking at each other hoping for the other to speak first.

He took a deep breath, broke the silence. "Capture them, take them alive if we can. Give us time to deal with Sorsha." He scanned the boardwalk to the building followed by the top of the wall. "If I fail, and...*she* comes for you. Launch nets into the air at the winged horses, bring the battle to the ground."

"That's one thing, but those stone giants she made will make short work of a net, or anything else I've seen here, *or* at Cherteri."

"I got an idea for them," said Thor.

"I hope it's a good one," Darla added.

Have faith, darlin'. But just in case you're not as capable as I was with her." Thor wrapped an arm around Darla's waist, puller her close, and smirked at Lucius. "Don't forget you've got a bargaining chip to get close to Sorsha." Thor pulled out his purse containing the other shard of Xanatos' amulet and tossed it to Lucius. "Do us a favor and keep it covered this time."

Lucius caught it, smiled, he wasn't sure if it was due to the gem in his hand or the thought of seeing Sorsha, getting close to her, with or without the amulet shard.

Thor nodded. "You got this."

"You too."

Thor leaned forward, arching Darla back, past her point of balance, and kissed her. "You come back to me," he said once he stopped, and righted her.

"And you stay away from those"—Darla glanced at Cinna then looked back at Thor— "women, else you'll learn I'm to be trifled with far less than any other woman you've met."

Thor simply grinned, nodded. "I shall try to satisfy your request."

Darla tilted her head, kissed him again, then turned for the gate, and left without another word.

"And you keep an eye on our gold." Lexa slid her palm down Eric's chest. "I didn't go through all the trouble of stealing it for you to lose it while I'm away."

"I helped in liberating said gold, if you recall."

Lexa kissed him, shoved him back. "And don't take from my winnings." She poked him repeatedly in his chest to every word.

Eric chuckled, shook his head, and looked to Lucius. "Just bring her back would you, and try not to spend a fortnight lounging around with Sorsha in Cap Canna once you've freed her."

"It is nice there," Lexa said, turning for the gate.

"Get out of here." Eric slapped Lexa on her rear. She looked over her shoulder, threw him a wink and followed after Darla.

"I'll bring her back," Lucius said, turning toward the boardwalk.

"You still owe me a drink Lucius—I aim to collect," Eric called to his back.

Lucius kept his eyes trained on the docks hoping he'd be enough to take down a sorceress with nothing more than who he was, no weapons, no tricks, just himself. He didn't turn around, all that needed saying had been said, except…he raised his fingers in the air. "You still owe me two."

Chapter Nineteen

Raven slid a stone along her blade, sharpening it to ensure no chip or crack existed. The task had become a habit over the years, not only to prevent a catastrophic failure in battle that could lead to her death, but also to let her mind wander, let her ponder her next move. On this eve, as the setting sun splashed the sky in violet and crimson, she contemplated the ship docking on the river just before the falls leading to the bay surrounding Cap Canna. Though silhouetted, shadowed by the angle of the sun, she recognized it to be the ship Lexa had fled on. The thought of Lexa's betrayal warmed Raven's chest, filled her with rage.

Raven stood from her chair on the balcony, sheathed her sword, and leaned on the stone rail. At this distance all she could see was a figure tossing a rope to her warriors on the docks. Warriors that took the rope and went about their business. Who else would be allowed passage but another sister? "Rejoice," Raven called out to women beside her on the balcony, within the main hall, on the beach. "Darla has brought me a prize."

"Lady Lexa?" asked a dark-haired warrior stepping up beside her.

"Her head," Raven corrected her. "Be a dear, fetch some wine and cups, would you, Sister."

"Right away, Raven." The woman bowed and left to carry out her order.

"And a pike for Lexa's head to rest upon," Raven added.

The air of the bay smelled extra fresh as Raven took a deep breath and watched a winged horse climb into the sky from the docked ship. The evening sun shrouding who she assumed to be Darla in shadow but left a menacing outline advancing toward her, a good approach to use in the future, she thought. Start a campaign with enemies in fear of what they cannot see clearly, as opposed to gracing their sight with the beautiful women Raven made her army from.

Raven waved, and the figure waved back. The winged horse set its hooves on the terrace, turning to let the sun's rays reveal its rider.

"It's good to be back here." Darla dismounted.

"Good to have you back. I trust you were successful." Raven gestured toward the cliffs. "Even brought back my ship. Not bad for just a serving girl."

"Past lives and all." Darla gave Raven a hug. "Thanks to you."

Raven didn't return the embrace.

Darla released her, and stepped back. "I had to travel far to find Lady Lexa. All the way to Tenzin." Darla furrowed her brow. "Do you know how many *men* are in Tenzin? Too many."

"We'll take care of that together, Sister. Your return is a good omen." The dark-haired warrior Raven had sent away returned, handed out cups, filled them with wine, and made to leave.

"Can you bring two more cups please, Sister?" Darla asked, and received a nod in response.

"A double-fisted celebration, or are we to have company?"

"You'll see." Darla winked.

Something wasn't quite right about Darla. A feeling that she was trying too hard to impress crept up within Raven's mind. Darla spoke in a tone more like her old self, before she was granted her gifts in the desert, she sounded as if she was back at the Feisty Goat catering to customers in order to fish another coin from a purse. Raven fancied herself more than decent at picking up on someone telling a tall tale, or withholding something.

"You haven't answered my question, and I don't see a sack dripping red with Lexa's head tied to your mount. Were you successful?" Raven's joy of her sisters' return quickly became overshadowed with doubt as Darla failed to answer without being asked again. Raven hated repeating herself, it was an annoyance she tolerated for but very few.

"Your orders were to bring Lady Lexa back to you in a bag, well I did one better. I brought her back in a boat, and I brought her back alive."

"Oh"—Raven looked to the ship, thoughts of prolonged torture ran through her head—"good girl."

"She has quite the story, you might be amused by it."

There it was again, a feeling of Darla withholding something. Speaking only in half-truths. "Have you grown soft in your time away from me? Presuming to know what *I* would like. *Your* Queen. And then telling me what I should do and who to listen to." Raven fingered her sword at her hip. "Measure your next words carefully…Sister."

Darla took another step back instead of speaking or reaching for her sword.

"Then there's that, your lack of spine. I'd have drawn on anyone for speaking to me as I did you. You're going to tell me what's going on right now before I—"

Great wings threw dust in the air as hoofs hit stone. Raven tossed her cup to the terrace. Her Sword sang as she freed it from its scabbard and turned toward the second winged horse to land on her terrace this eve. Side stepping to keep one eye on Darla, Raven held her free hand to the sun silhouetting the mount's rider as a handful of her warriors surrounded the winged horse.

As if Raven willed it, the horse turned to let the sun's rays illuminate it, and its rider. Correction, riders. The mount carried two, Lexa dismounted without a word. The man did the same, and his presence took Ravens breath from her chest.

Lucius, her beloved Lucius, had returned to her.

No, it can't be.

Raven locked eyes with him, eyes that seemed to smile at her, that told a tale of safety, a tale of passion to come, a tale of love. Hope welled inside her. She tried to speak, but no words came forth.

Darla held up her palm. "Better than a sack tied to my mount, yes?"

"Beloved?" Raven stepped forward, finding her voice, ignoring Darla, Lexa, and the sisters at her side. She had to refrain from trembling, from letting her eyes water.

How could he be alive? He was buried under the mountain, or so Thor had told her.

Lucius's gentle smile, his slight nod, tore any questions from her. The how didn't matter. He was here, once again by her side, the only man she deemed worthy of her heart, of her body, of her bed.

Her sword fell to the cobbles, her heart sped, as did her pace as she moved to touch him, to embrace him. A man of not only many words but words filled with wit said nothing, there was no need. His arms pulled her close, wrapped about her waist. His lips, soft and warm, pressed against hers. Heat flushing from her head. She pulled away from his kiss, buried her head against his chest, and heard his heart thudding within. "You're alive." She murmured.

"And right where I'm meant to be." He stroked the back of her head, tucked her hair behind her ear, lifted her chin, and kissed her again.

She accepted it, shuddering, her hands shaking beyond her control, and she became aware of it, of the eyes on her, judging her. Raven pulled back, steadied herself, and addressed the women surrounding them. This man is my prisoner, and is not to be touched by none other than myself. Escort him to my private chambers at once."

Raven's sisters hesitated, but the two closest to Lucius stepped forward, their hands on their hilts. One reached for Lucius's arm, stopped herself, looked to Raven, then held her hand out motioning the direction Lucius was to take.

Lucius frowned and shifted his eyes, looking over the women. His face softened, relaxed. Raven had seen that look on him before. He understood when to act, when to speak, and when not to. He walked where he was directed, winked at her as he passed her by, and disappeared from sight through the main hall's doors.

On this eve she got more than she could have ever hoped for, though she still had her image to portray, her queendom to rule, and her subjects need not doubt her devotion to them. Lucius was hers once again, and she would not lose him, nor would she lose all she'd built. "That man,"—Raven pointed through the doors—"is from my past, the one that aided me in bringing down the Last Atlantean. For his crimes of being male he should be turned to match his brethren, but through his actions I was granted the opportunity to be your queen, the opportunity to free all other sisters in the world. For that reason, and that reason alone, I grant him a pardon from transformation or death. He will spend the remainder of his days in servitude to me."

Nods were the only reply from her sisters. They may not agree with her, but she would not be challenged. Lexa and Darla, on the other hand, looked confused. Lexa squinted, her mind processing all possibilities, as Raven had come to know her to do.

Darla had an err of fear about her, shirking away, shifting her gaze to the cobbles. These women, especially Lexa, had been with her since the beginning of her quest, but they disobeyed orders, and that could not be tolerated. "As for Darla and Lexa"—Raven intentionally left out the *Lady* part of her name that the sisters had become accustomed to—"Take them to the dungeon. Feed them, do not abuse them." Raven picked up her sword, let its blade scrape along the stone as she approached before pointing the tip at the two women. "I shall deal their punishment firsthand."

Eyes widened before her, but only on Darla. Lexa retained her composure as always.

Raven spun on her heels, strode for the main hall, knowing her order would be carried out. "Fill your cups, Sisters. This eve's events are truly worth celebrating."

Raven did her best to strut with confidence, and not sprint to her bed chambers, to Lucius.

Chapter Twenty

Lucius, escorted by two women clad in armor bearing the Raven's crest, was led inside a large room filled with tapestries, a bed, chests, and a fireplace. The matching ornate carved wood of the bed windows and chests told him he was in a king's chambers. It weighed on him, as he struck a fire, how Sorsha had changed. His companions had told him of her change, but he wasn't prepared for what he saw, or heard. Her dark armor, straight black hair, deep purple paint around her eyes, none of it resembled the woman he'd come to know. The cunning, the guile, the commanding presence, those he recognized, and for a moment, in their embrace, he *felt* Sorsha within the woman he held. He might be enough to pull her free of Raven's grasp. After all, Thor did it, and Lucius was always a believer that if one man could do something then so could he, and he could probably do it better.

He paced round the room as the black of night overtook the sun's final rays, contemplating how he'd approach her, how he'd remove the amulet from her flesh. He'd left his collapsible bow, quiver, and sword on the ship as per Lexa's warning about how he would be received. She was right to be cautious, as she always was, but he did risk keeping his knife.

Fortune smiled on him when Sorsha…Raven ordered the warriors that brought him to these chambers not to touch him. If they couldn't touch him, they couldn't search him either. He thumbed the tip of the knife's handle, protruding, yet concealed to be part of the clasp on his belt. Though the blade was only thumb-length it could be deadly, and it had the added benefit, from being so small it fit in the palm of his hand without non being the wiser. He almost pulled it out and palmed it but decided if he needed it to scrape the amulet from Raven's chest, he should first glimpse it, get a feeling of its angle, its depth, its edges.

"Leave," Lucius heard the commanding voice from the other side of the door say. "There's no need to stand guard. Go enjoy yourselves, Sisters."

Footfalls sounded, fading to the distance. Then the door opened, and in walked Raven. She turned her back to him, shut the door, and above the crackling of the fire Lucius swore he heard the latch on the door slide in place, sealing them within.

They wouldn't be disturbed, and they were alone with no aid on the other side of the door. Lucius couldn't help but think that the opportune moment was presenting itself. He'd use is wit, his banter, and hopefully their embrace to try and pull Sorsha's mind free of the Raven's grasp. Barring a failure, he'd wait till she slumbered beside him, in his arms, and would separate her from that cursed amulet shard.

Raven unclipped the clasps on the side of her armor and lifting it above her head, turned toward him. As her breastplate fell to the floor, Raven changed, and transformed before his eyes in a single wave. Her dark armor remained unchanged, but her straight black hair brightened, and became curly red locks. The violet paint around her eyes turned to a smoky gray, and her lips brightened to a deep crimson. The woman before him, now resembled the woman he'd come to know, come to want to spend the remainder of his days with, and as she slipped her undergarment over her head, he saw the means to keep her that way. The amulet shard shimmered as eerily as the first time he'd seen it, teeming with sorcery. He focused, concentrating his gaze on Sorsha's face. She swayed her hips, dropping her leather skirt past her greaves, and kicked it to the side.

Naked aside from her bracers and greaves, she charged him, shoved him to the bed, and pressed her lips to his, hard.

~*~

The moment Sorsha finished, she shuddered and collapsed atop him. Spent, she let out a deep breath, kissed Lucius ever so gently, and climbed off him to lay at his side. She traced her fingers across his sweat-beaded chest. She'd put him to the test, as she had before, and like before, he passed. Satisfied, her primal urge met, she made for a table, picked up a jug of wine, and drank deep, spilling drops down her chin to her breasts. She picked up a cloth, turned back toward her beloved, and began wiping the wine and sweat from herself, studying him.

Sorsha smiled at Lucius as he looked her over. He couldn't contain a look of lust even after what she'd just put him through. He mustn't be as spent as she thought he should be. She stood beside the bed, and spoke the first word between them since she entered her chambers. "Drink." She hoisted the jug above his head, tilted it, forcing Lucius to open his mouth and catch the wine trickling down. She poured what he could take, set the jug on the tiny table beside the bed, gently toweled the sweat from his chest as he cleared his throat, and climbed back in bed, pulling him back down to let her rest her head in his chest. "I thought I lost you."

"You nearly did." Lucius wrapped his arm around her, squeezed her tight. "But in part you hastened my freedom from the mountain."

"How's that?"

Lucius reached down, pressed his thumb against the amulet shard embedded in her chest. It tingled as if he was connected to it. Sorsha gasped then covered her mouth. His flesh had a grayish undertone. She'd witnessed Xanatos sap Lucius' soul from his body as he protected her from suffering the same fate. It didn't bother her, his coloring, all that mattered was that he was here beside her. Now, she wondered if the reason the amulet reacted to his touch was because *he* was in it, his soul. Could she somehow give it back to him, make him whole? Making a mistake when dealing with sorcery could be life-threatening. Wouldn't it be better to have him alive the way he is? Besides, she had no idea how she could perform such sorcery. Sure, the amulet was one with her, but it was no more than a shiny…trinket.

Sorsha rolled away from Lucius and cradled her head in her hands, straining to recall how she got where she was, what she'd done. It was like a foggy dream, hard to recall what was real and what wasn't. Had she changed, truly changed? Not how Lucius had, but differently? She was the Raven, had been for years, but since the battle at the mountain she was…different. She used to be *the* Raven, the most feared mercenary leader in the land. Now, she had *become* Raven. Had lost herself to the amulet's power?

"Oh Lucius, what have I done, what's become of me? It's like I was fighting in Xanatos's lair…then…I'm here. Racing toward you with only one thing on my mind. But, there's part of me that…that…"

The bed shifted under his weight as he pushed himself up behind her and ran his hand up and down her back, assuring her with a touch that she needn't find the words. She was a fierce warrior, strong willed like no other, yet she felt as confident as a wee child.

She felt scared.

She turned back to him, putting her palm on his cheek. "At least I got you out…the other side of me…"

"As it was when we met, you have a hold on me. It's just a little stronger now."

He always knew what to say, and how to say it, to lift her spirits, to engage her wit. Her first meeting with him came to mind, and how he'd spoken of nothing but dancing and good times to be had with her, with not a mention or hint of bedding her as all other men did upon first setting eyes on her.

"I would have found you sooner had we not gone the wrong way. Perhaps I could have pulled your mind back to you days ago, as it is now. Had I known I would—"

"We?" Sorsha cut him short. "Who else made it out with you?"

Lucius dropped his gaze. Sorsha knew the answer before he said it, thus the reason for him averting her eyes.

She answered her own question. "Thor. Thor survived." His name on her lips flushed her cheeks. Suddenly she became embarrassed of being naked. She covered herself with her arms, stood, and stomped over to her garb. "That oaf. That barbarian made it out. You're…changed. I sure am. And he's walking around, probably with our gold, no doubt wasting it on lines of harlots."

She had tested Thor, to see if he was worthy of her bed. She'd sent Darla to him, paid her to bed him, and he didn't hesitate. Thor failed her test, but it was more than that. He enraged her. His tactics, his sharp tongue, his brazen outspoken manner, everything about the man pissed her off.

"I suppose next you're going to tell me that scoundrel cousin of his is by his side."

Lucius remained silent; he was hesitating. Looking over her shoulder she saw his nodding her correct assumption.

Rage boiled up in her, and she needed to let it out. Screaming, she hammered her fist into the table. A pop sounded; pain shot up her arm. She'd broken her hand before, punching a pig of a man in the forehead, and this felt the same as it did then.

"Will I ever be rid of that cursed family?" She scooped up Lucius's tunic, hurled it at the wall in a final fit of rage. His purse flipped free from the tunic's folds, spilled its contents on the floor. The gem in her chest warmed, tugging at her flesh as if trying to pull itself toward the other shard. "What…have you brought me. Another piece of…" Sorsha breathed deep, dug her nails into her palms ignoring the shooting pain from her one fist.

"I found it," Lucius said, standing from the bed. "In Xanatos's lair, on my way to you."

Sorsha silenced him with a hand in the air. She stepped closer, felt the pull of the crimson stone shimmering on the floor. It moved, by itself, sliding toward her, as if it wanted to, needed to, yearned to be whole again.

Lucius' shard flew through the air, slammed into the one in her chest, dropped Sorsha to her knees, and the world fogged over in a violet haze once more.

Chapter Twenty-One

"Launch," Thor ordered the half dozen citizens of Raich charged with manning that particular catapult. Its arm swung through the air, stopping with a thud against a leather-wrapped crossbeam, hurling a stone at its target.

The head-sized stone crashed through the roof of the last building prior to the open expanse between the city walls and the boardwalk. "Back it off three notches and fire again," Thor called out from the top of the wall.

"You'd think these things had never been used," Eric said.

"I think you're right; it was hard enough to find guards that knew how to run them properly. Never mind teaching the people of Raich." Thor said as another stone flew overhead to land in the grass ten paces from the outlying buildings. "Good, now back it off another two and fire again. Do the same to the others and put a stake in the ground where the stone lands. Not where it stopped but where it lands, so one of you get out there."

"And keep your head up," Eric added to Thor's command who in turn gave him a scowl. "If I don't say it, they'll be busy digging a hole for the corpse instead of working the next catapult. You know I'm right."

Thor grinned at his cousin. "Always got the answer, don't you?" Before he let Eric retort, he ordered the men below once more. "When that's done back it off another three pegs and stake the position. The first stake will mark the point for stone and silver, the second stake, the one further out, will mark where the jugs of oil will land. Mark each catapult well so as not to get confused in the battle. Be ready, else the hesitation get you killed when you're thinking about which to load."

"You would have made a great lieutenant, captain even." Eric turned to face the northerly wall.

"Tell me about it."

"A captain of babes still on the breast, I mean. We're all doomed." Eric grinned.

Thor swung his fist at Eric's shoulder. His cousin backed, spun, and took off in a sprint. "It's a good thing your fast, cousin," Thor murmured, giving pursuit.

He chuckled, as he ran, at the frowns of the men he was commanding. The game he played now was one he and Eric had rehearsed many times. Eric's mouth would start it, and Thor's fists would end it. He looked at each round as a lesson, training his younger cousin for fights he would surely get into. It was rare Eric could beat him exchanging blows, but over the years his cousin had grown skilled, landing decent hits. But, unlike today, Eric was never able to outpace Thor. He cursed the furry side of his cousin, giving him the advantage to pull away so easily. He pushed himself to speed along the top of the wall faster, but only caught Eric because he slowed, stopping to contemplate something with a puzzled look on his face as he stared at the armaments surrounding the northern catapults.

"The pebbles?" Thor asked following Eric's gaze below, guessing that's what had Eric vexed.

"What are you planning to do, bruise them to death?" Eric motioned, indicating the baskets laden with tiny rocks.

Thor slapped Eric on the shoulder. "For the giants."

"What?" Eric said, rubbing his shoulder.

"Think of the stones we tossed down by the river when we were boys. Small stones chipped and cracked the bigger ones. And what happened when we struck the stone surrounding a fire-pit that's been blazing?"

"They split open."

"Same thing here. Just the big stones are walking now. Pelt them with pebbles, crack 'em throughout, cover 'em in oil."

"Light 'em up." Eric nodded. "Launch larger stones afterward."

"Now you're getting it. But let's see if you're learning anything from this captain of babes." Thor pointed his thumb over his shoulder. "What do you think I have them doing?"

Eric turned, studied the scene of townsfolk digging in the dirt. "You got me, what am I looking at?"

"Guess you'll find out when the battle is upon us, Lieutenant." Thor grinned, punched Eric in the shoulder, and took off running.

Eric shouted at his back. "You know you can't outrun me now, right!"

I can still try. Thor leapt over the side of the wall dragging his dagger down its face to slow his descent. He kicked off the wall to change his trajectory from a straight drop to land on his hands and roll up to his feet. He made it two paces, and Eric's feet hit the ground before him. Thor lunged forward, driving his fist into Eric's gut, doubling his cousin over, and skidded to a halt. "You may be faster, but I was always the better fighter. Wolf or not. I still am."

Eric groaned, stood. "But not even *you* can take on an army of those like me, and that's why I have to go."

Thor's grin vanished as he knew what his cousin meant. Never one to be a coward or shirk from a fight, they both yearned for the greatest adventure's the world could throw at them. "You're gonna try and turn them back."

"I have to try. It's because of me that they're cursed."

"No, it's because of Xanatos." Thor corrected his cousin. "Cursed us all in one way or another. What we've got to do is accept it and move on. Unless we can figure out how that amulet works, or convince Sorsha to use it and reverse what Xanatos did. This is who we are now." Thor held up his clenched fist and stared at it as he worked his fingers. "This healing thing has come in handy. I don't feel as bad sending you to the flat of your back."

"You never did."

"Might be just what we need if Lucius fails to free Sorsha. That is if separating her from the stone will even work."

"It's all a gamble."

"So, what's new?"

"Us, and your right, we gotta do what we can with what we got. Who knows, I might become the Alpha of the pack."

"There you go again thinking you're the best at something."

"Well, as of right now, I am the dominant species." Eric raised his chin.

"How's the gut of the *dominant species*?" Thor asked, not expecting a reply. They stared at each other a moment, grinning as only cousins could do at an unspoken bond. "Let 'er buck,"—Thor slapped Eric on the shoulder hard enough to make him shift his weight—"Alpha."

Eric rotated his shoulder. "You know I will." He hammered a fist into Thor's chest and sprinted away.

"Good luck cousin," Thor said, knowing his words would not reach Eric's ears. There was no need for more talk, they were both men of action. Looking over the people struggling to operate the northern catapults, Thor shook his head as he approached to correct their mistakes. *We won't last long fighting on two fronts if you can't pull of something cousin.*

Chapter Twenty-Two

Lexa squinted, tried to shake the spray of the river from her eyes. Again, she tested her bonds on her wrists, elbows, waist, and ankles, strapping her to the bowsprit. She'd seen ornately carved figures, mostly of women, where she hung from at the bow of the ship and thought it to be another form of being put to the question. Never did she think she'd find herself in this position. Aside from being soaked, and the chaffing of the ropes, she would have found it more tolerable had it not been from the spray repeatedly obscuring her vision.

Their journey back to Raich was sped along far faster than when she'd made the trip herself zig-zagging against the river's current, all thanks to Raven's sisters. Lexa spat water from her mouth, silently cursing the women standing on the bow above her, mumbling. Whatever Raven had done to them, she also graced the sisters with power to not only control the wind, but the water as well, propelling them toward their destination.

She and Darla had barely spent a turn of the glass in the dungeon before Raven gave the order to have both her and Darla bound to individual ships. They'd sailed the rest of the night and into the day with Lexa at the forefront of Raven's fleet. Craning her neck, she gauged the sun to be well past its zenith. Darla, she hadn't seen, but guessed she was strapped to the nearest ship following Raven's flagship, following her lead.

Lucius hadn't suffered as torturous a fate as her and Darla. While they were being escorted to the docks, Lexa overheard Raven giving Lucius his orders to put his skills to work at designing adaptations to the ships bobbing in Cap Canna's Bay. Massive whaling ships that Raven had commandeered from an attack by the people of Zorin. "Though seaworthy to hunt the great whales, these ships must be rebuilt to survive the harshest conditions the sea can throw at them. They must be made to ensure a successful journey beyond the waters man knows, and outfitted with enough supplies to sail for a fortnight or more, along with all that need be loaded to start anew and settle on virgin land."

Raven's command to Lucius had been far less cryptic than when she laid out her plans before Lexa. Growing her suspicion that something truly terrible was to come to pass, something Raven and Darla, and possibly the sisters, knew about. Lexa couldn't help but wonder. Was the world, the one she knew of, doomed to follow in Atlantis's footsteps? Why else the need for Lucius to redesign the ships? Why else would Raven speak as if she and her sisters would never return from their voyage? Raven had said that *this* was not her kingdom, and that more sisters needed to be liberated for the journey to come.

Lexa had plenty of time to ponder these questions. Unfortunately, she could only come up with one conclusion. The world, as she knew it, would come to an end. How? When? She didn't know. But it seemed as if Raven did, and it wasn't far off. Three times she'd heard the order, watched as a winged horse departed for Cap Canna with Lucius's drawings. Instructions for the sisters left behind as to how to rebuild the ships anchored there.

One thing was for certain, Lexa thought as she glimpsed a pair of riders speeding over the horizon toward Raich, if she was seeing shouts then she would be in the thick of battle within the turn of a glass.

~*~

"Thor, our scouts return!" called an archer atop Raich's wall.

Thor broke his conversation with Cinna short, looked to the direction the man pointed—east. He ran up the stairs to the foot walk to see for himself. The scouts galloped, pushing their mounts hard. If Lucius, Lexa, and Darla had been successful, his trio of companions would have been returning with Sorsha on a single ship, and there would be no need for scouts to be returning as they are. One word ran through his mind, though he dare not say it aloud; invasion.

Cinna made his way to the foot walk, leaned over a stone tooth, squinting toward the horizon. "You see anything? Are they back? Did it work?"

Thor watched the man display his unease. Cinna wasn't battle-tested; not like he was. Thor doubted from how the king of Raich fidgeted and kept glancing back to his castle that he'd ever been in a fight before, let alone a battle. Some kings are born with such luxury that guards took care of any issues for them, and Thor guessed Cinna was one of those kings.

"I doubt whatever they're coming to report will bear any good fortunes." Thor looked over the catapults, the men stationed around them, watched as some panicked, hastily double-checking their position, the ammunition, rambled with each other over controls. He'd done what he could to prepare these men, and true some were hardened, but others would not fare well should an enemy breech the walls.

"What if—"

"Don't do that. Don't question the men's abilities or yours. Guessing what is coming will only grow an unwarranted fear, letting the imagination run wild. All we can do is wait, hear what the scouts have to say, and go from there."

"I should warn my daughters, the people."

"They'll know soon enough." Thor turned from the king, made his way along the foot walk to stand above the gate.

Cinna rushed behind him, as if proximity to Thor might save his life.

The scouts rode up.

"What is it, men?" Cinna didn't wait for them to come to a stop before questioning his scouts.

"A fleet of boats, my king," one of the scouts pointed. "A dozen or more fishing vessels. All with decks full of winged horses and...huge...things."

"Things? What things, man? This is no time to speak in riddles." Cinna waved his hand about, wildly.

"Stone giants?" Thor asked the Scout, who seemed to think about the question, then nodded his response. "How soon?"

"Can't say, they're...making the river...push them here, against the flow. Won't be long."

Thor had previously ridden to where the scouts were posted. A full turn of the glass, maybe more, Thor thought. That would be the time they would have if the ships moved up river by normal means. Now, with sorcery upon them, they would have to make haste. "Get your men to positions, Cinna. Sound the warning bell. Get everyone within the walls as we've planned."

Cinna looked to the archer beside the warning bell. "You heard him. Sound it."

The archer dropped his bow, picked up a hammer, let it ring off the bell.

Those who hadn't heard the archer's shout about the scouts returning heard the warning. People scurried through the streets before the wall, gathering what they deemed necessary, and rushed to the gate. Word had been spread. They knew what to do, they knew of the potential threat, and that every last one of them might be needed in the battle. Still, with all the warning and preparation, Thor watched as more than one person was knocked down or shouldered aside for being slower than the rest of the people scrambling to get within the walls.

Raich was a peaceful town, one that Thor couldn't recall hearing of even having skirmishes with neighboring kingdoms. Though its people may have never been put under siege, they would stand a chance, because they would stand. He could see it in their eyes, not all of them but most. A look not of fear and desperation, but one of determination. In all his years Thor had witnessed many battles. The thing that never ceased to amaze him was how merchants, farmers, fishermen, even stable boys, could show more courage than trained armored guards if backed into a corner.

From the far end of the city, the other warning bell was struck. Thor dropped his gaze, hoped the man ringing the far bell was just repeating what the archer beside him was doing to spread the word. But he knew better than that. Communication was key to survival. The men on the walls, though perhaps not battle-tested, would be trained to sound only one alarm, the one closest to the threat. Cinna looked at him, his eyes wide.

Thor raised his hand, counting his finger-breadths between the sun and the horizon. There was less than two turns of the glass left before they lost the light, lost advantage of sight. And if Eric too has failed, Raich may not be standing come sun up.

Then it hit him, he'd expected and prepared for a land attack, but if Raven had a fleet of ships pushed forward by sorcery, then they might not be able to avoid a collision with a vessel speeding toward them by means of the river's current. If he loosed every fishing boat Raich had, let them float toward Raven as fast as the river can carry them, the result could be catastrophic to her fleet. At the very least the collisions and guaranteed debris would ensure Raven's fleet would have to make landfall prior to reaching the city.

Thor ran down the steps, barking orders as he went. "You, you, and you. Follow me. Make haste."

"Where are you going?" Cinna called down to him.

"To send every boat Raich has down river!" Thor shouted, not looking back as he ran to the docks.

Chapter Twenty-Three

Lucius finished marking up his final design in his book. Normally he'd have taken greater care, and time, to sketch every fine detail of his designs. Rough outlines by his stringent standards, were all he'd produced thus far, and those had been whisked away back to Cap Canna by women on winged horses so construction could begin. But what he just completed; he spared no detail. He'd noted everything required to alter Raven's flagship, right down to pin size, placement, and the material it was to be made of to secure the alterations to the largest ship in the fleet. This was to be the one Raven would lead her sisters from. This is the one he ensured would be the most steadfast of them all. Be it he succeeded in separating Xanatos' amulet from Raven's chest and restoring Sorsha to her normal self, or he failed to do so and she remained the Raven, he would not let her perish by a faulter in his craft.

In truth, he admitted to himself as he shut his book, slipping it in his pocket, he'd immersed himself in his work to keep his mind from replaying the night before, when his piece of the amulet merged with the one in Raven's chest. It broke him, to watch helplessly as Sorsha transformed before his eyes, changing into the Raven. Her physical appearance was one thing he could handle, after all, women had a tendency to alter their hair frequently, both in style and length, along with their face paint. What he had trouble coping with was her mind, and how she shifted from the woman he cared for to someone he barely recognized.

His work complete, he set to recalling every detail of their embrace, and every pass of his fingers over the amulet. It was indeed one with her, no ridge, no edge, nothing presented itself as a finger hold to grasp the shard and pull it free from Sorsha. A knife would be the only way, he decided, especially now that the shard had more than doubled in size. He thumbed his concealed knife. Pondered how, in the midst of the coming battle, he would create his chance. Turns of the glass were running out. He might have to act even with Sorsha surrounded by her warrior women as he'd not been alone with her since she absorbed the second amulet shard and reverted back into being the Raven. The coming battle would have to be used as his distraction. When Raven's Sisters would be deployed, he would have to act.

"Are my plans complete?"

Raven, interrupting his thoughts, pulled him back to the moment. Even now, with her clad in black, he felt a pang in his gut at the pain he must inflict in the woman standing above him. Her fists on her hips, her hair and cloak swaying with the unnatural wind, and her icy glare, all forged a persona of someone not to be trifled with. But he was never one to shirk from prodding a mind, pushing it to the point of confusion.

"For a ship to be fit for your command, and seaworthy, yes. But adapted to be worthy of your presence on board, darlin', not as of yet."

Lucius paused, waited for a reaction. Flattery, he knew, was at times as useful as a flower when it came to setting maids off-balance. The same was for Raven. He caught her glance at him, momentarily, as if he were still beneath her in the bed chamber, before she returned to studying the horizon. Whishing he was, he stood, followed her gaze, and continued to press her; knowing what Sorsha truly desired. "Your personal touch is what I require to complete my design. Captain's quarters set for two—"

"Two?"

"Of course, I still owe you that dance." Lucius stroked his chin, feigning deep contemplation. "Or was it you that owed me? Either way, a queen needs her privacy, and room to move about. You know, ponder her next move." He held his hands before him spreading them to the sides. A grand map wall, one to replace a clunky old table, allowing for greater ease of planning and making room…for…whatever a queen might desire."

"You would presume to know what I desire, would you?" Raven's gaze had yet to shift, though her tone wasn't as sharp.

"No man should ever presume to know what a woman wants," Lucius said, catering to Raven's ego. "He should ask. And if she graces him with truth, he should do what it takes to fulfill those wants."

He tapped his book bulging the pocket on the side of his breeches. Stepping before her, forcing her to lock eyes on him, he took her hand in his, bent low, and kissed her knuckles. "What do you wish for, my dear?" He couldn't bring himself to call her Raven, and he thought calling her Sorsha would hinder any softening of her stern composure. Her hand tightened on his, gently, almost lovingly, then fell sharply to her side."

"Blood is all I want."

Raven stepped past Lucius, though her words were perplexing her fingers tracing over his as she went made Lucius consider he might be getting through to her. He turned to follow her lead to the bow and froze.

Ships, boats of every size, littered the water's surface around the bend. Each one flowing with the current, unmanned, and speeding toward them.

"Cowards!" Raven shouted, then turned and stomped along the deck. "Setting such a thing at me…no honour…no fight…just gutless, pig headed tactics. Well, they do not know who I am, nor who I command."

Lucius moved to the bow, and the bowsprit, giving Raven room to move, room to rant to herself among the women waiting her command.

"Sisters of the sea!" Raven called out, raising her hands in the air. "Clear us a path!"

Raven must have read the confusion on his face, because with one look at him, she took Lucius by the shoulder, turned him to the lumbering boats coming their way. In the water Lucius caught glimpses of flowing hair, scales, and fins as they appeared then sank beneath the river's surface, speeding faster than their ship could move; sorcery or not."

"See," Raven whispered in his ear. "Blood shall be mine."

Chapter Twenty-Four

Thor climbed the massive swing arm Lucius had designed for their ship, grasped the top, and leaned, squinting to see if his plan worked. The boats he'd set free would crash into Raven's fleet and send at least one to the bottom of the river.

His grip tightened. Every boat, no matter the size, lurched to the side, propelled by an unseen force to the river's bank, clearing a path for Raven's fleet. "Sorcery," he grumbled.

Something caught his eye, something more than the flicker of the sun on the water's ripples. Something moving against the current. He climbed down as fast as he could, leapt to the deck, ran to the rail with sword in hand.

A thud hit the hull, followed by another.

Thor looked over the rail to find two women, naked, bobbing in the water. On a different eve he would have found such a sight enticing, but not with sorcery in the air. More women appeared, and as one they pushed against the ship.

Thor laughed, producing scowls on the women's faces. "You may have pushed those fishing boats aside, but you can't really think you can capsize this ship." Thor shook his head, Xanatos may have created creatures the likes of which he'd never seen before, powerful ones. But if this is the best Raven can send his way, naked maids, victory would be his, and he would fulfill his oath. The giant stone men Lexa spoke of might be cumbersome, useless in a fight, if these maids were any indication of the battle prowess Raven bestowed on her creations.

Wood snapping sounded from below him. The creaking, cracking, of boards echoed from within the hull. Then he saw it, below the water's surface, each woman was armed with a blade, and they were using them to pry at the hull.

The gold.

Thor contemplated jumping into the water, but he'd be outnumbered by far, and should he win the battle he could always reclaim that which sinks to the riverbed. His years in battle had served him well, and brash decisions making had slain many a man before their time.

He left the women to their work, to stripping him of his fortune, and ran for the castle wall.

From atop the foot walk Thor watched as the great arm Lucius designed to wrench stones from the river sank beneath its ripples. He'd won and lost fortunes before, one never as large as what was stowed on the ship, but gold was useless if a man wasn't alive to spend it. So, he turned his attention to Raven's fleet, shoring up to the river bank.

The lead ship was the first to make ground, and he guessed that was where he would find Raven. Squinting, he saw larger than normal beings disembarking from the other ships, the ground forces. Women, not naked to his disappointment, mounted winged horses, the areal forces. More women, all donning armor matching Sorsha's and those on the winged horses filed into formation behind the stone men.

From the formation, and from his experience fighting with Sorsha by his side, he guessed the stone men would be set loose as the first, expendable, wave of attack.

Sorsha, rather Raven, stood on the flagship's foot walk commanding her troops. Lucius was at her side. He didn't appear to be bound, but he wasn't making a move to stop Raven. Had he given up? Had he not found the right moment to strip Raven of the amulet? Had he tried and failed? Worse yet, had he taken the amulet for himself? If so, Thor could be up against not one but two forces controlling Atlantis' sorcery.

He pushed the questions aside, there was no place for them. Soon enough he would find his answers.

Thor searched, but not one of the other women looked familiar, until he studied the flagship closely, along with the ship next to it. Lexa and Darla were each tied to the bowsprits. They were brought down and strapped to the chests of the stone men. Arms and legs spread wide, Lexa and Darla were meant to fall by his sword. Raven's tactic was one he'd seen before, one used to drive despair into men's hearts. Force an army to slay their comrades lashed to whatever an advancing enemy chose to attack with. Be it wagons, ships, or even the protection of catapults, the tactic worked. Men would not loose an arrow at their own. But women lashed to massive stone abominations, no matter how arcane the sight, would force an even more effective deterrent.

Loud and clear he heard Raven shout the order, "Destroy the city!"

He was right about her battle plan, the stone men started their advance first, followed by the women a good hundred paces behind them, each bearing a sword, bow, and quiver.

It will be a battle of arrows, Thor thought, guaranteeing Lexa and Darla's deaths.

Thor sighed, looked to the men ready at the catapults, the king by his side, the archers lining the foot walk.

There was only one thing he could do.

"Follow the plan, Cinna. But try to spare those two." Thor pointed at the bound Lexa and Darla being led helplessly their way.

"What are you going to do?" King Cinna asked.

"Save my friends."

Without another word, Thor left the safety of the castle's walls for the unprotected, unwalled part of the city. He ran down alleys, streets. At every corner he stopped, peered to see where the enemy was, and signaled back and forth to Cinna guiding him to his targets.

Cinna barked orders; oil jars soared overhead followed by flaming arrows.

The giants had reached the first markers. Thor had to hurry.

Black smoke rose above buildings indicating where the oil was lit, and Cinna, though directing his men, guided Thor to a patch of clear sky between smoke trails.

Stone slamming against stone echoed down the abandoned streets, off the walls. Rubble crumble to cobbles followed, putting speed to Thor's legs. He rounded a corner, skidded to a halt before Lexa, and her stone captor.

"Thor!" Darla shouted from her own stone captor beside Lexa, her voice filled with excitement and a hint of panic.

Sword drawn; Thor made ready to leap clear of a stone fist thrown his way.

The creature before him raised both fists, dropped them into a clay roof, sending clay shards raining down to the cobbles. Thor backed, looked to Darla and her captor. It did the same.

"Would you get us down from here?" Lexa called to him.

A stone foot tore through a smith's shop, littering the cobbles with bits of steel, hammers, and other tools. Raven's command, "Destroy the City." These things followed her orders all right, they were laying waste to the city, not its people.

Thor chuckled. His fortunes were improving.

He leapt up, slashed at the rope binding Lexa in place.

Her ropes unravelling, she swung down, landed on her feet.

"Dumber than the ones at Cherteri, aren't they?"

"Good thing too, it took you long enough." Lexa stepped aside, making way for her massive stone captor to continue its onslaught of the building.

"Could have left you," Thor said to Lexa as he maneuvered around Darla's giant for a clean shot at her restraints. "You *did* look as if you were faring well on your own." He grinned, slashed Darla free, and caught her in his arms. "Miss me?"

Darla planted a kiss on him, a hard one, then pulled back. "The sisters won't be as easy to deal with."

Baskets of rocks and pebbles flew overhead. Cinna was following the plan, pelting hot rock with stone. The rocks skipped, bounced, nicked, and cracked, off the stone giants, but they pressed on crashing through houses and shops.

"That's not going to stop them," Lexa said after shielding herself with her arms from the stones ricocheting back at them.

"No, it's not." Angered more than disappointed that his plan for the giants failed, Thor motioned Lexa and Darla to back and away from the lumbering behemoths. "If we don't come up with something else there won't be a city left standing. For now, they're of little threat to us."

"You're right, but *they* are." Darla pointed to the winged horses riding high into the sky above them.

"Not to us, the city." Thor backed into the shadows, studying his adversary above. "We have the advantage. We've gone unnoticed. No troops come our way save for these stone creatures. We make for the docks, wind our way round, come up behind her."

"Stay clear of the water, though."

Thor couldn't have asked for a better companion for his plan, he thought, watching Lexa scoop up three blades from the fallen smith's shop, inspect them, weighing them, and checking their balance despite being void of finished handles. Her skill with throwing knives was unmatched, and her stealth gained through thievery would not hinder him.

He pulled his dagger, gave it to Darla, and turned for the dock mooring Sorsha's ship.

Chapter Twenty-Five

"Men!" Sorsha shouted, throwing her arms up, pacing on the deck of her ship. "Even as bumbling piles of stone, they can't listen. How am I supposed to liberate my sisters from those infernal cousins if the troops under me can't think to attack the people in the city and not just its abandoned shanties?" Raven looked at Lucius shrugging his shoulders. "Look who I'm asking, another man…thick-headed…sons of…blot out the sky with your arrows!"

Raven's warriors mounted on winged horses took to the air, climbed above the city, arrows notched, loosed by her command. Though bounding up and down, her sister's aim was deadly. Archers fell, tried to return the arrows sent their way, but her sisters flew high—Raich's arrows would not reach them.

Nets soared through the air, clipping hooves, missing their mark and falling to blanket the ground.

"This won't take long," Raven said, grinning as some of her stone men reached the castle wall, pounded on it. "Come,"—she motioned to Lucius—"see first-hand how those fools fall."

She disembarked, letting her ground forces do their part. To her surprise they did more than loose arrows waiting for the giants to punch holes in the wall and clear a path for them. Her sisters had truly been gifted, and she saw the shock of it on Lucius's face. "Like what you see? Aren't they gorgeous, utilizing the talents I bestowed upon them?"

For once, Lucius had little to say, he just took it all in, his eyes wide. She let him enjoy the spectacle, the balls of fire formed in her sister's palms, the gusting wind hurling the flaming orbs, fueling them. Slabs of rock pushed up through grass and dirt, forming shields that absorbed shrapnel sent her sister's way; shield that pushed forward with every advancing step.

"Glorious, but not as terrifying as it should be." Raven raised her palms to the sky, concentrated, felt the pull, the power, and unleashed it where she pointed.

Lightning surged, cracked the dark clouds she formed, and struck whatever it found on the other side of the wall.

Raven drank it in, eyes shut. The screams, the cries for aid, the arrows whooshing down, the stone crumbling, the crackling fire consuming the city. The scent of smoke filling her chest brought visions of charred men lying dead, littering blackened cobbles. She fingered the amulet—now twice its original size—felt its warmth, its surge of power, and its inhabitants. She felt Lucius, part of him within it, and it welled in her, the only man her former-self deemed worthy of her *was* hers to command for all time. He would not disobey, he would only do as commanded, as she wished. He would be her slave, the only man to settle the new world with her sisters.

"Tell me." She commanded of him. "What hope is left for the city, for the *men* dwelling within?"

Lucius clenched his jaw, fought to withhold his thoughts, but ultimately let them pass by his lips. "Me."

He lunged, tackling her to the ground, muffling her words with his hand clutching her mouth.

Clever, she thought, even as they tumbled, rolled, and grappled for control. Her former-self had chosen wisely. Strong, fast, and bearing enough wit to silence her commands—he impressed her even more. She let him pin her, amused at where he thought this would go. With but a word she could stop him, if she could slip an audible one past his palm, but what could he do to her? His grip was tight, but not enough to bruise, his fists did not rain down, and his eyes…his eyes told the tale of a man tormented, of one not willing to harm one who held his heart. She felt a tugging, almost a stinging pang in her gut, deep in her chest beneath the amulet. Did she still care for him? No, she decided. Memories of a past life. He was no more than a plaything to her now, one to bed, feed her grapes—in silence—once he'd satisfied her.

A blade no longer than her finger flickered in his palm.

"Forgive me," Lucius murmured as he slashed the knife down.

Searing burning pain filled her mind. Her body locked, stiffened, as if trying to fend off the attack by cocooning itself.

The world glazed over in a crimson hue, her inner power instinctively encasing Lucius. The blade slicing the amulet from her flesh pulled free taking the stinging pain with it. Lucius's touch was non-existent. His legs straddling her, his iron grip on her wrist, his palm on her mouth—it was all gone. Lucius hovered above her floating, immobilized as with crimson tendrils seething over his entirety.

"How dare you." Raven flicked her hand and sent Lucius to the grass beside her, pinning him down and spreading his limbs wide.

The blood on his blade, her blood, enraged her.

"To think I was going to grace you with the honour of servitude. And how do you repay me?" Raven gingerly caressed the amulet, the wound beneath it. Slick with blood, her fingers worked the gash, healing it. "Betrayal, that's what." She said to herself as she shifted her attention from Lucius to the carnage laid down by her sisters. "They're all I have that are loyal now."

The city had all but fallen, her ground troops were within its walls, her air troops circled above in an endless loop of death raining down arrows. Smoke licked the sky, obscuring the sun's setting rays silhouetting a lone figure on the horizon. Raven focused. Who would be so brazen to oversee the battle? The man let out a battle cry as he charged toward the city. Though too far away to clearly make out his features there was a familiarity in his voice, to the way he moved.

"Eric," Raven sneered. "I welcome you to your demise."

Raven looked to the sky and concentrated, thickening the clouds above the city. She would cook Eric with a single strike and leave him to be no more than a charred, smoking, husk.

The battle cries of hundreds of men following Eric's lead over the hill, charging the far side of Raich's remains, tore her attention from above. He'd raised an army. Impressive, but it would fall just as easily as the one her sisters smote down within Raich's walls. The final rays of the sun blinked out, and the battle cries from Eric's forces shifted to that of agony as they collapsed to the ground. Not certain of what caused them to falter Raven almost let herself revel in the sound of tormented wails, but she had to be certain Eric and his force would not stand again.

After what felt like a turn of a glass the cries of Eric's force subsided. Eric was the first to rise from the silence. A howl cut through the night as he continue his charge forward on all fours. Her sisters would have to deal with an army of wolves.

Chapter Twenty-Six

Lexa ducked, crouched, crept through the rubble that used to be the outmost dwellings and shops of Raich. Eric's howl, the force he commanded, couldn't have been better timed to allow a thief to close in on her target. Thor had taken Darla by way of the river's edge to close in on Raven. Whereas she had decided, mid-route with Thor and Darla, to flank Raven from her left. With Eric's pack battling Raven's ground and air troops pouring out the city at her back, Lexa had gone unnoticed, of that she was certain.

She closed in, fingering the blades she'd found, wishing they were hers, the ones she was used to. A glance to her left told her Thor was making as much progress as she, even with Darla trailing him. Raven, stomping toward the chaos, was almost close enough to be hit with a throwing knife. Lexa dug in, pressed up against the remnants of a wall, and waited for Raven to get close enough that she might leap out at her, catch her off guard, and carve the amulet from Raven's chest.

Raven struck lightning at the land, the city, Eric's pack, with no regard for her sisters. Friend and foe fell on the far side of the city, though the wind hadn't brought the stench of burned flesh to Lexa yet, she was prepared for it.

She peered around the wall, vexed, her heart broken to see up close just how much Sorsha had transformed into the Raven. The amulet, she could see, was larger than before. Lucius's piece was now one with Raven, feeding Sorsha's insanity, and power. Her control of Lucius following behind her like a dog was disheartening. Lucius had failed, more than once. His bout with Raven didn't last long before Lexa heard Raven command him to never attack her again. Had she been closer, Lexa would have charged into the fight, aided Lucius, but even an all-out run wouldn't have gotten her to them before Raven tossed Lucius aside and took control of him. The fact that he was still breathing after such an attempt did give Lexa hope that Sorsha was still within Raven, fighting to stay her own hands from slaying Lucius.

Raven screamed, pointed, and lightning scorched the rubble, close enough Lexa jerked from the impact. Eric had abandoned his pack save for six wolves that followed him, charged on all fours beside him directly for Raven.

This was what she needed, a distraction like no other, and close enough to Raven that it kept her full attention.

Lexa scurried, crouching behind a fish market's remnants, flanking Raven, keeping from sight.

"Why won't you die!" Raven shouted toward Eric and from her palm sent a crimson ray of light his way.

The light didn't char stone, as Lexa expected, but utterly destroyed it, along with two wolves not as fast as Eric was at leaping to avoid the blast. Though not close enough for her liking, Lexa knew she had to act now, else the man she loved would suffer the same fate.

Lexa stood, charged forward, and caught Raven's attention. Another beam meant to obliterate the wolves moved with Raven's hand, surged toward her. Lexa tumbled, rolling to avoid it, let it pass above her head. The stench of burned hair filled her chest—*that was close*. Lexa pressed on, batted Raven's hand aside, sending the murderous light to carve a hole in the captain's quarters of Raven's flagship, nearly killing Thor racing toward them.

Lexa made to put her shoulder into Raven's gut and tackle her to the ground, but pain struck her neck and the back of her head during midleap. She collapsed to her knees; her vision blurred—she wanted to empty her stomach. She'd caught the pommel of Raven's sword, Lexa guessed, in the head, and the blade was sure to come next.

Lexa rolled, clumsily, to the side fighting to stay awake. She glanced to Thor, still a good dozen paces away and out of reach to come to her aid. Raven towered above her, poised with her sword held high to strike a killing blow. Lexa raised her blade, preparing to deflect Raven's sword. Though unlikely to succeed against Raven's skill it was the only move Lexa had left. Out of the corner of her eye, as Raven's blade surged down at her, Lexa saw Thor raise his sword high overhead with both hands and hurl it toward them.

"No!" Lucius cried out, leaping between the spinning sword and Raven.

He collapsed to the ground beside Lexa, with Thor's broadsword in his gut.

Raven ceased her death blow mid-stroke at seeing Lucius. Her sword fell to the ground as she dropped to her knees beside him. Raven leaned over him, rocking back and forth with her fists pressed to her lips. She dropped her fists to her side and screamed skyward.

The ground shook beneath Lexa.

Dirt and stone rippled out knee high around the three of them like waves. Each crest shot debris into the air, peppering Thor and Darla with the first wave and knocking them to the ground. The earthen waves pressed on to Eric and the remaining wolves, stopping their assault.

The ground cracked open around Raven as she cradled Lucius, pulled him to her, and lifted them both on an earthen pillar high above Lexa's throbbing head. Lexa clambered away, blocking stones tumbling down from the pillar.

Eric scooped her up, growled at the four wolves, sent them climbing the dirt pillar, clawing their way to Raven and Lucius.

He bounded back, carrying Lexa to the ruined city. She tried to focus, to clear her head, her vision of the crimson overtaking the night. It wasn't her eyes, she realized, it was Raven sending out power, pushing them all away, forcing them back.

They flew through the air, shot like an arrow, and fell. Rolling, Eric used his massive body to shield hers. He craned his neck, as did she.

A crimson dome surrounded Raven and Lucius, had stripped the land smooth for a hundred paces, sent them back to the outer limits of the ruined city, along with all its rubble.

Eric slashed a claw at it, pounded a fist against it—the crimson dome flickered but didn't falter.

The roar, the constant drone of the battle in the distance ceased, paused for a moment, then began again with shouts, cries, and howls retaking the night, closing toward them.

Lexa looked for Thor and Darla. The pair of them, along with Raven's ships, had been forced to the far bank of the river.

"Oh, Eric." Lexa reached up, ran her fingers through the fur on his shoulder. "What are we going to do?"

He wrapped his claws, gently, around her neck, holding her head up, and stroked the back of his hand down her cheek as if to say it will be alright, as if to comfort her. But Lexa knew it would not be all right. What was to come she couldn't even guess. They can't get to Raven, no one can save for Lucius, and his wound looked fatal.

Tears ran down Lexa's cheeks. She forced herself not to give up, not to lose all hope as she wiped them away, tried with all she had to compose herself, to recover from the blow she'd suffered. She let him pull her to him, let him press her against his chest, doubting she could rise to her feet under her own power without falling.

A scream cut through the night, through the dome, from Raven. Her cry was one of torment, utter pain. Lucius was dead, Lexa guessed, and with him all hope for Sorsha, or them.

Eric lifted her, turned Lexa so she could see.

Raven was on her knees atop the dirt pillar with one hand pressing Lucius's face against her chest as she cradled him against her. She was vibrating, shaking her free hand clenched in a fist at her side.

The crimson dome flickered, shrank back to Raven, then surged outward away from her back toward Lexa and Eric.

Dry searing heat slammed into Lexa as the dome approached. Eric crouched over her, wincing as he shielded her from the heat. Crimson flashed all around them, strafing the land at their sides as the dome raged past. Lexa's arm around Eric's back shrieked at her. She shuddered and pulled herself into a ball as Eric covered her with his body.

As fast as the dome was created it was gone, as was Lexa's arm below the elbow.

Her breath short, her body shaking, Lexa clutched at her charred stump.

Eric released her and coughed out a mist of blood as he collapsed to his chest, twitching. The entire back of his body that shielded her was void of fur. Caked, crusty, burned flesh was all that remained between blackened ribs and shoulder bones.

Lexa took his hand in hers as she lay back. She gasped and let her eyes fall shut, certain they would never open again and the last sight she would befall is the base of Eric's exposed skull.

Chapter Twenty-Seven

Sorsha wept, her body trembled, exhausted. She'd won. She'd pushed Xanatos' tainted version of the Raven back into the amulet. The power unleashed during her internal battle unleashed a wave of devastation, but it was nothing compared to the devastation she felt within. Using the amulet's power seething through out her, she lowered the pillar of earth to the ground as she cradled Lucius. Then willed her appearance back to the woman Lucius had known when they first met.

His grip, strong despite his wound, held her tight. "I found you."

"You did," Sorsha said, wiping tears from her face, trying to be strong for him.

"Knew you were in there. Just wish"—Lucius quivered, clutched the blade in his belly—"it happened sooner."

Sorsha took hold of the broadsword, gripping the blade above Lucius's blood-slicked hand. "Ready?"

Lucius nodded. Sorsha heaved the blade free, tossed it aside.

Lucius convulsed, coughed.

One hand pulling him to her chest, the other covering his hand on his wound, Sorsha pushed power through her, drew it from the amulet, forced it into her beloved. "Stay still." She held her voice, nurturing, untremblingly as possible, and reached out with her mind, with the amulet's sorcery…her sorcery.

Close it, heal it, seal it shut, make it good as new.

She tried, with all she had, all the power seething within her…but the wound refused to obey.

"I can't…"

"It's okay." Lucius stared up at her, his brilliant eyes filled with pain.

If she couldn't heal him, perhaps she could lessen his burden. She reached out again, this time to his mind. She felt his pain, as if the gash that opened him was her own, right through to her lower back. A cold sweat overtook her as she willed the pain from her beloved, sharing the burden of what was to come.

Lucius took a breath, deep, and full. "Thank you."

A tear spilled, not from the pain she shared with him, but from the agony in her heart. She would not waste his last moments with words that need not be said. She pressed her lips to his, memorizing them. Their warmth, their soft gentle touch, the scruff of his beard irritating her face that wasn't there the night before. She pulled back. "I love you." She managed to get out, not letting her voice crack.

"I know," he jested, smirking, prompting a grin from her. "And I you." Lucius slid his hand from his hold on the wound, wincing. Sorsha held hers firm on it as he dug in his tunic, produced his "book of scribblings" as he had once called it. "It's finished, it's sound, it will not falter no matter what the sea hurls at you." He pressed the book against her.

Even at his end, he was thinking of her, caring for her, ensuring her survival. Her tears ran unchecked, but she didn't sob. Her tears he deserved, like no other in this world, but she would hold herself together, she decided, and show him her love, her passion, not her fear, her dread, her lack of control.

"And I have something for you, beloved."

Lucius cocked his head, perplexed yet full of wit, contemplating, as she'd seen him do time and again.

Sorsha took a deep breath, filled her chest with the cool of the night, and searched, searched for him, her lover. Lucius's presence, his essence, his soul, rose up, separating itself from the others contained within the amulet.

She pressed her lips to his again, breathing not life, but his soul back into him.

Sorsha released their embrace, watched his skin. Though covered in dirt and his own blood, his color returned to him, driving every hint of gray away.

Lucius shuddered, drawing air. "Thank…" he shuddered again, murmuring on his final breath. "You."

Sorsha stared into his eyes, watched the light fade, the spark dwindle. She let go of his wound, wiped the blood from her hand on the dirt, and gently slid her fingers over Lucius's eyes, shutting them.

She broke, inside, sobbed as she pulled him to her, wrapped herself around him. How cruel of life to have let her finally find a man worthy of her heart only to strip him away? She was responsible, as much as the blade that took him, for his demise. No…not her…not the blade…him…Xanatos.

"I vow to you, beloved," Sorsha whispered in Lucius's ear. "Your sacrifice will not be forgotten."

Sorsha laid Lucius on the ground, kissed him one last time, and kneeling beside him, she dug her fingernails in her own flesh, and tore the amulet free from her chest.

Chapter Twenty-Eight

Thor emerged from the river and sprinted over scorched earth leaving Darla as sopping wet as he and trailing behind him. His dagger at the ready, he prepared to leap over his fallen friend, and lunge at Raven, burying his blade to the hilt in her heart. But the shock of crimson hair waving in the wind, the scream echoing through the night, and the amulet skipping along the dirt slowed his pace.

Sorsha had freed herself from the grasp of the Last Atlantean.

He knew it, just from the look of her, she was herself again. Panting, and on all fours, Sorsha collapsed to her side, her hand on Lucius's chest. His friend, his cellmate, was gone, killed by his doing, but Thor didn't regret his actions, hurling his blade at Raven. She was lost, from what he saw. How not even Lucius could reach Sorsha within the Raven, how Raven subdued him, enslaved the one man he thought had a chance at setting her free. He knew he had but one chance to end Raven's tyranny, and he took it. He didn't think Lucius would sacrifice himself to save her though. He regretted losing his friend, but not his decision. Now he regretted slowing his pace as Sorsha caught sight of him, pushed herself up, bearing his broadsword that had ended Lucius's life.

Thor weighed his options and decided to let Sorsha make the first move. His guard up, Thor came to a stop just outside striking distance and waited silently. If her glare could cut him down, he would be dead before his corpse hit the ground. Fierce and full of rage, more than he'd ever seen before, Sorsha stood her ground, guarding over Lucius's body.

She stepped around Lucius, keeping her glare locked, and stuck her face in Thor's. A handsbreadth from each other, she could not utilize his broadsword, but a dagger, of which there was no doubt Sorsha had, could strike a killing blow from where she stood, especially due to her battle prowess. He can heal, and would heal from any damage Sorsha could inflict with a dagger. The question was what to do with her if she tried. Did he take the hits? Let her vent then restrain her? He certainly did not want to cut her down now that she was herself again, or so he hoped.

Footfalls, and heavy breathing behind him, told Thor Darla had reached them.

"I would have done the same." Sorsha turned, slammed his broadsword into the ground, left it swaying back and forth and went back to Lucius.

A warrior like her, Sorsha would not speak of what transpired again, the battle sure, over wine, but never the pain, the anguish filling her. Thor wrenched his sword free, wiped it clean and sheathed it, then got down on one knee beside Lucius's body. "It's done," he said with a nod, then pulling out his purse and spilling the gold, he plucked the amulet from the dirt, concealing it in its soft leather home.

"We're going to need that," Sorsha said, indicating the amulet as she picked up Lucius's book, tucking it snugly under her belt.

"Have you gone mad?" Thor cringed at his quick tongue. Of course Sorsha had gone mad, but was she still? "This thing belongs at the bottom of the sea."

"I'm sorry for your loss, but Thor's right Rave...Sorsha." Darla pointed to the city. "Look around, they're still killing each other over there."

"We need it, but not to stop them, I'll explain later." Sorsha spun, strode for Lexa and Eric. "Right now, we need *him*."

Thor glanced to Darla, considered pressing Sorsha further, but knew what she was getting at. Eric was the only one who could control the pack of wolves. If Sorsha's forces combined with what remained of Raich's people can't bring them down, they'd be over run. He kept pace with Sorsha, and for the first time since she'd reverted to her old self, Thor laid eyes on his cousin.

He ran, outpacing Sorsha and Darla, dropped to his knees beside Eric. His cousins' breathing was laboured, but he lived. Thor placed his palm on Eric's pink back. Warm to the touch and void of all fur, Thor guessed Eric would pull through thanks to his curse. Whether he could be roused to command the pack was unknown.

Thor looked past his cousin to Lexa, and seeing her limp body, the charred stump where her arm used to be, and the blood seeping between blackened flesh, he feared the worst for her. Eric had taken the brunt of Raven's attack, and was indeed healing at a rapid pace despite being unconscious, but Lexa's condition was far worse.

"He lives, good. Rouse him," Sorsha said to him as she knelt, pressed her ear to Lexa's chest. "She's alive,"—Sorsha ran her fingers through the blood pooling beneath Lexa's stump— "I can't say for how long."

Thor watched, as Darla placed her palm on Lexa's cheek, a nurturing touch. And how Sorsha tore off a strip of her cloak, tied it just above Lexa's elbow, then squeezed her eyes shut, and covered her mouth with her hand. She did this, caused this, all of it, yet she held her composure. She was a fierce warrior, hardened not only by battle but the tragedies of life. In truth, he admired her more than when he sought employment with the fabled Raven. He'd only know the tales of the Raven's exploits. After discovering Sorsha was the Raven, going to battle with her, and against her, he felt a sense of pride for her. Honorable, he thought, it just panged him that such a companion would spend the rest of her days haunted by her actions. Though her wits were overtaken, the actions were still hers, and thus the burden as well.

Thor looked to the city, the flames flickering on either side of its walls, the shadowed, silhouetted figures tearing at each other. Aside from the women on winged horses, it looked as if the wolves were winning, surging with sheer might and ferociousness through those mounting a ground assault. If they were all Raven's warriors, Raich's, or a pairing of them both he couldn't tell. He assumed they would cease fighting each other to take on the wolves, but a dagger in the back of even a temporary ally is tempting. He'd been at the pointed end of such a dagger in his youth and knew how quickly alliances shift in the midst of a blood-drunk rage.

Eric was their only hope.

Thor hefted his cousin, rolled him up to sit with his massive head hanging low. Grabbing Eric's maw, Thor shook his cousin's head. "Eric, you must wake. Wake!" He shook him harder, faster, but no sign of Eric rousing showed.

Sorsha cut another strip from her cloak. "I'm sorry old friend." She wrapped Lexa's stump.

Lexa didn't move, didn't moan, didn't twitch. Thor feared she was to far gone to be saved. "This night's toll is heavy. Come on, Eric." Thor shook his cousin by the shoulders, slapped his snout. "Wake!"

"It's no use," Darla said, wide-eyed, looking toward the city and the swarming pack advancing their way. "We have to flee…make for a boat if there's one left." She whipped her head around searching the ship's debris in the distance.

If there was one still seaworthy, it might be their best chance, Thor thought. But Raven had splintered many ships in her final showing, and he doubted they'd find one intact. He shook Eric harder.

"There might be another way," Sorsha said to them, then rummaged through Lexa's robes, and smiled. "Leave it to a master thief to be prepared for anything."

From the fold, Thor saw Sorsha produce a leather pouch the size of his hand. Hardened and form-fitted like stubby fingers, he knew at once what Sorsha was looking for, and had found. Oils derived from plants with various functions.

"Question is, which one?" Sorsha unfolded a flap, revealing five glass vials held in place, each one with a different colored liquid in it.

"Look for one with bone shavings in it." Thor stopped shaking his cousin, held Eric steady with one arm, and reached for the pouch. "One with brown, yellow, or clear water in it." That much he knew.

"What is that?" Darla asked.

"A waking potion," Thor answered.

"More sorcery."

"Far from it, Darla." Sorsha pulled a vial out one at a time, found one matching Thor's description. "Boiled crushed up hooves or antlers mixed with herbs, catch the steam and it makes the potion. Like a good thief, Lexa would have kept the shavings in the bottle for easy identification."

"It's not widely known," Thor added. "But it works."

Sorsha popped the top, waved the bottle under Eric's snout.

Eric jerked, tossed Thor back, and knocked Sorsha to the side.

Shaking his head, snorting, he took in those around him and braced himself on all fours, his claws digging into the dirt. He settled his glare on Lexa.

Thor and Sorsha exchanged glances, neither sure what Eric would do.

Eric winced as he moved to Lexa, sniffed her stump, pulled her limp body to his massive furry chest, then snorted and huffed at Thor. His barreled chest rose and fell as he looked from Thor to Lexa, then to Sorsha and Lexa again. Eric raised his snout, huffing once again, spraying mist from his nostrils.

"He wants us to wake her," Thor said, keeping his gaze locked on his cousin.

Eric bobbed his head repeatedly.

"Stop them first." Sorsha commanded, pointing at the carnage taking place in Raich.

Eric followed her outstretched arm, craned his neck turning his head to the side, then howled to the night sky.

The battle at Thor's back shifted, the screams of death and chaos diminished and were replaced with a brief lull before being renewed with cheers. The pack of wolves had ceased their onslaught and began to retreat. The cheers were cut short by the stark battle cry of a woman.

"Enough!" Shouted Sorsha. "Stand down!"

Thor watched as the closest of Raven's warriors to them, still being a good three hundred paces away, heeded the order.

"Stand down!" Sorsha repeated.

Her orders sounded from her force's troops, repeating from ground to air, the message was made clear, and the city of Raich fell silent. Be it in confusion or in elation Thor couldn't tell, but he didn't care. The battle was one, and there was only one matter left that needed tending to.

Thor gently coaxed the potion from Sorsha's hand as she glared over her troops, then waved the bottle under Lexa's nose.

Chapter Twenty-Nine

Lexa cringed, snorted and coughed at the sharp stinging assault on her nose shooting up her head, a sting that paled in comparison to the agony coming from her arm. She was weak, as though she hadn't slept for days, she focused on her arm, and gasped.

There wasn't much left of her arm below the elbow. No hand. No wrist. Barely four fingerbreadths of her forearm remained, blackened and charred, with her lifeblood seeping through pink cracks and dripping down a singed bone protruding from her stump.

This is it; my fight is over.

A hand caressed her cheek, lifting her gaze. "Lexa," said Raven, speaking softly.

Lexa pulled back as best she could, more shirking her head and shoulders deeper into…Eric's massive arms, his crimson eyes large as ever staring down at her.

He's alive. Still protecting me.

Lexa looked back at Raven, her hair had changed from straight black to flowing crimson locks, her darkened face paint gone, her armour altered to reflect the true Raven she once was. She stood within arm's reach with a softened expression on her face, and a gaping wound where the amulet shard once was. "Sorsha?" The name croaked from Lexa's dry throat.

"It's me, thanks to you." Sorsha smiled with her lips, but not her eyes.

Thor appeared beside her, kneeling, holding up a wineskin.

Lexa made to reach for it, instinctively moving her stump less than a handsbreadth, and paid for the motion with searing pain shooting from her mangled limb up to her shoulder. She squeezed her eyes shut, forcing tears from her watering eyes to streak down her face. She breathed deep, opened her eyes to Sorsha holding the wineskin just before her lips. She tipped it for her, sweet wine spilled into Lexa's mouth.

My last drink.

She swallowed, hard.

With friends.

She nestled her head against Eric's furry chest.

And the man who holds my heart, still on guard, still by my side.

"It's okay," she said to him. Her voice was less parched, more like her own, though weaker than normal.

"I wish that were true," said Sorsha, her eyes locked, her composure steadfast. "We have a chance, but I'll need you by my side if we're to survive."

"Not sure I'll be of much use." Lexa coughed.

I don't have the strength to stand, let alone fight. I'm so tired.

"We have to leave the world behind, sail for the new one," Sorsha said, standing.

"The world has been mapped." Thor said. Lexa couldn't help but notice he pivoted his weight to an alert, defensive pose. "You're saying you want to sail off in hopes it hasn't been. That there's land beyond the furthest ships have been able to reach?"

"It's not a *want*, we have to." Sorsha stepped back.

A writhing ball of mist formed between the three of them. Sorsha was mumbling something Lexa couldn't understand.

Every drop of moisture in the air gathered to form a giant ball. The air took on the smell of the desert, dry, mixed with the overwhelming taste of scorched earth. "Cherteri, Raich, Cap Canna." Sorsha stopped mumbling just long enough to speak actual words.

The floating ball of moisture thickened and shifted to display each city with condensed water as she spoke their names, each surrounded by landscapes of either mountains, rivers, or desert. Lexa recognized them, and the accuracy matching maps she'd studied in the past. Sorsha had retained some of her sorcery, perhaps all of it, and appeared to have control over it.

Darla stood poised, and silent. Eric tightened his grip on Lexa ever so gently. Thor had his hand on the hilt of his dagger, Lexa wondered where his weapon of choice was, his broadsword, but dismissed her pondering; not believing she'd live long enough for it to matter. Sorsha's display however, though it be sorcerous, was amazing to look at.

The water droplets zoomed out. "The world as we know it," Sorsha said.

The seething water showed everything, from where Atlantis fell on the west coast of the world, past Cap Canna, all the way to Morrin in the far-off east.

"The world as it is." Sorsha spread her arms wide, and the ball of water zoomed out again.

Lexa couldn't help it, wanting to discover this new world Sorsha was showing them. What she knew, what everyone knew to be the entire world, was just an island. A small one in comparison to the massive land formations spread across the ball Sorsha had created, each having terrains as varied as the ones Lexa had studied on what she once considered world maps.

"You know this how?" Thor asked, almost glaring at Sorsha. He had a hate for sorcery, as did Lexa, but he was holding his ground, and his tongue.

"The amulet. It showed me. Showed me what we didn't know. Showed me what's really out there, beyond what the greatest ships have discovered. More importantly it showed me that the sorcery Xanatos used to plunge Atlantis into the ocean still stirs and will soon bring the rest of the old world down to join that damned city."

The world Lexa knew, that she'd studied on maps, sank beneath the writhing water of Sorsha's ball. Sorsha mumbled the water back to moisten the air it had come from, though it did little to lessen the scent from the scorched earth Lexa lay on.

"How do you know this to be true?" Thor questioned Sorsha, stepping forward. "And even if it is, no ship can cross such an expanse of ocean, if your...drawing is accurate." He waved his arm at where the floating ball of water had been.

"It's true, I've seen it." Darla put her hand on Thor's shoulder. "More like I've felt it, felt the land tearing itself apart. We must make haste."

Finally, they're cryptic speak has ended.

Lexa dropped her gaze. All the days she'd spent wondering what Raven and her Sisters knew, that knowledge, has finally been spoken of with a normal tongue.

Eric snorted, swiped at the dirt beside him, and held out his clawed hand bearing a strip of cotton half charred on either end. Lexa grinned. Though not yet back in his true form, she had reached Eric once more despite his curse. His gesture, small as it was, meant he understood they needed to leave. Perhaps he felt the same kind of pull Sorsha and Darla had. Either way, him presenting his cotton belt cocooning the feather she had given him on their first night together, Lexa took as a sign, a sign he cared deeper for her than she ever imagined.

"I'll never make such a journey, even if you can reach land," Lexa said, fighting to stay awake.

"We can make it. We can survive the journey. I've no doubt." Sorsha pulled Lucius' notebook from beneath her belt, held it up. "My beloved ensured we could with his designs. And you have to make the journey. I'll need this child's aunt if I'm to raise him properly." Sorsha slid her palm over her belly. "I can't do it alone."

Lexa teared up as Sorsha's words settled in her, as she looked around to find Thor's broadsword standing in the dirt, and beyond it the motionless Lucius. They'd not carried him with them, to her. Surely they would have done so had he been alive. Sorsha was herself again, free of the Raven. Lucius must have succeeded in his task, and not only devised a means to save her from the coming catastrophe but left Sorsha with the greatest gift of all before he perished; the child growing in Sorsha's belly.

"Oh Sorsha. I'm sorry." Lexa's tears ran unchecked. She was weaker, could barely raise her one remaining hand. She looked at Eric, wishing he was himself for one final embrace before her breath left her. "I'm sorry." Her head fell back, heavy, into Eric's arm.

I won't make it.

She tried to say more. To tell them more, tell them how she felt truly about them, her companions, her friends, and her lover. No words passed her lips. She couldn't move them enough to speak. Her eyes became tired, and she wanted to sleep. Slowly, she let them fall closed, listening to voices speak words she couldn't make out, along with a howl.

Her body twitched, pitched upward, and pain tore into her throat, her shoulder, made her cringe as if she'd been stabbed by multiple knives, and forced her to glimpse the world one last time. She drew a shuddered breath and let her eyes fall shut, as her lover sank his fangs deeper into her body.

END OF BOOK TWO OF THE CRIMSON SERIES

Made in the USA
Monee, IL
13 September 2024

64774091R00080